WHAT EVER HAPPENED TO JO ROSE?

CHRIS DILEO

Grindhouse Press #103
ISBN-13: 978-1-957504-16-2

For Carrie Nicely and Marissa Rantinella

Also by Chris DiLeo

"Come, you spirits that tend on mortal thoughts, unsex me here, and fill me from the crown to the toe top-full of direst cruelty."
—Lady Macbeth,
The Tragedy of Macbeth

"You *should* be afraid of old women."
—Josephine "Jo" Rose

"I could've been one of the greats!"
—Helga "the Hag,"
What Ever Happened to Helga the Hag?

PART ONE:
HALEY AND MS. ROSE

1

I WAS A QUIET GIRL who read books and wrote stories in glittery pink journals, and then one night I was the young woman with her boyfriend's scrotum in one hand and a pair of red-handled garden shears in the other.

2

I WASN'T LOOKING FOR A job when Emma mentioned Ms. Rose. I already had a job at the Warrenville Library. Not much—minimum wage for twenty hours a week, re-shelving books, updating library cards, waking the occasional afternoon napper—but it was quiet and undemanding. And I had plenty of time to read and write.

Besides, I love books.

That day I was reading *Slaying the Masculine*, a guidebook for "women trying to survive in a man's world." Most of it was bullshit, though probably not as much as I wanted it to be.

Today's man is the legacy of yesterday's brutal conquerer.

Beneath that caption was a cartoon Conan-type muscle-bound hero in a loincloth and brandishing an enormous sword, but this Conan was standing by a water cooler declaring to a woman in business attire, *I declare myself man!*

"Hey, Haley," Emma said. She was good at sneaking up on people, especially me whenever I was reading, but I didn't let on that she'd startled me. It was especially impressive because her music, some mix of shouting female and shredding guitar, whined through the pink Beats headphones around her neck.

She leaned over the circulation desk, her shirts always low-cut, elbows on the counter, chin in her hands. "How's the box?"

Code for *What's up?*, *How's everything?*, the question was an inside joke going back ten years since the sleepover in middle school when we cocooned ourselves in a comforter and secretly watched a '70s horror movie called *Cabin Girls* Emma's dad had on VHS. In it, a deranged man sexually torments women in a woods-engulfed cabin. Throughout the movie, the gap-toothed and drooling psycho rapist taunts each victimized woman, *How's the box?*, meaning of course her privates and this was so disturbingly hilarious we've never stopped quoting it.

"Tight," I said. Which is what the Final Girl says each time she's asked and the last thing she says just before she finally kills him.

In her best throaty hillbilly psycho voice, Emma said the response: "I like 'em tight."

"I bet you do," I said and looked back down at the book. *To get what you want in a man's world, you must think like a man.*

An adjacent cartoon showed that business-clad woman wielding an enormous sword of her own and proclaiming, "I am woman!"

Interestingly, the cartoon business woman's blazer had lost a button because of her suddenly mountainous breasts. The cartoonist must be a man.

"What're you doing?" Emma asked.

We readers know when asked such a stupid question the asker isn't looking for an answer. They're seeking our attention.

I turned the page.

"Oh, maybe you didn't hear me." Emma exaggerated a loud cough and said in a Broadway voice, "Excuse me, dear librarian, can you tell me where the *sex* books are?"

Typical Emma. Her flair for the dramatic, and her love of attention, had her belting out Taylor Swift songs in our high school cafeteria, soaking up all the downstage light she could in every school production, making TikTok videos in gas station snack aisles, and blurting all things sex-related in preferably inappropriate places—college lecture halls, grocery store checkout lines, and here at the library where I worked.

I closed the book and Emma leaned over farther, going up on her toes.

"I don't need your boobs in my face," I said.

"I'm proving a point."

"About your boobs?"

She glanced over her shoulder, which pulled her shirt open

3

enough to expose the triple-moon tattoo below her collarbone. Emma had said it was a symbol of feminine power.

I didn't have any tattoos, my skin as virginal as the rest of me.

Beyond the circulation desk was one of the Quiet Study areas, four long tables, straight-back chairs, green bankers' desk lamps. Two people were at different tables, a middle-aged woman with her glasses pushed up on her head and two stacks of books around her at one and my boyfriend, Colin, at another reading a magazine. At least looking at the pictures. He glanced over.

He wore his high school letterman's jacket, football, which since he wasn't in high school made him sound like a pathetic, dumb jock, but he was smart(ish), gentle, sensitive, and cute, a great smile and a head of hair always appealingly uncombed.

"What point?" I asked.

"Wait for it," Emma said and leaned toward me even farther as if to whisper something.

Colin's eyes widened.

In one smooth gesture, she slipped the headphones off her neck and plopped them over my ears. The music was loud and sounded like thousands of rats squealing inside a collapsing building.

Emma grinned at me, licked her lips, and pushed out her jean-clad butt in a slow erotic sweep.

Over her shoulder, I saw Colin mesmerized by my friend's butt.

I yanked off the headphones and Emma leaned close as she could, extending those long legs of hers. "He's looking, isn't he?"

I didn't respond. *A man is a little boy with adult desires,* the cartoon Conan book said.

Emma turned to give Colin a naughty boy back-and-forth finger.

He saw me seeing him seeing Emma and almost fell out of the chair flinching back to his magazine.

"See?" Emma said. "Can't be trusted."

"*You* can't be trusted," I said.

"I'm your best friend. I only want what's best for you."

"That's why you ask about my box?"

"Isn't that what men do, ask each other how their dick's hanging?"

"I wouldn't know."

Emma took back her headphones.

"You wear those when you're checking patients' vitals?"

"Makes it easier to give them a show." She swivel-popped her hips.

4

"You actually like that banshee music?"

"It's feminine power, baby." She worked her hips again and slapped her thighs.

"Stop. You're in a library."

She slouched on the counter. "What's your boy toy pretending to read over there, anyway?"

"Sports. Cars. Something."

"Porno?"

"We don't carry porn."

"They even make those magazines anymore? Isn't that what we call 'problematic'?"

"He's not reading a porno."

"Well, no," Emma said, watching him turn a page and then another, "he's not reading at all."

"Be nice. He's trying. He's a good guy."

Emma patted my head. "So innocent. There's no such thing as a good guy."

"What do you want?"

"It does bring up an important question," Emma said, channeling her inner-therapist voice. "What flavor of porn is his favorite?"

"Ew."

She counted on her fingers. "Barely legal, MILF, spinner, lesbian, jerk off instruction, domination, bondage, cum slap—"

"*Stop.*"

"I bet he likes the stepsister ones."

"I'm going to puke."

"That's a category, too."

"Are you here to annoy me?"

"That's what friends are for."

"Friends are for helping one another."

"Read that in a book, did you?"

She tried to see what was on the page.

Men are pure ego. Cartoon Office Conan headed out of the office with the woman slung over one shoulder and a donut raised high in his other hand. He declared, *I want so I take.*

I shut the book, pulled it under my arms. "Fine. You have my undivided attention."

"That's a good girl. I got a job for you."

3

WHAT SHE MEANT WAS SHE wanted me to do her job.

After only one semester, Emma dropped out of Binghamton and moved back home. She enrolled in nursing at the community college. At the same time, she volunteered with a local organization that helped people in need, everyone from victims of domestic abuse to elderly people living alone. Which is how Emma met Ms. Rose, a seventy-something former actress living by herself in an old Victorian in town.

She'd visit her every night—making her tea, listening to her stories, helping her get ready for bed, and so on.

Emma soon made her nursing focus eldercare.

"You really want to take care of old people?" I asked her. This was back in January. We were eating fries at McDonald's. Snow swirled across the window.

"Old people are the best," she said.

"Bed pans and dementia?"

"I thought I was the cynic. Old people have *experience*," saying the word like I'd never heard it. "And they can be a real hoot."

"A hoot?"

"Yeah, like Ms. Rose. The shit she says."

"Like what?"

"Religious stuff."

"Super-Christian?"

"Definitely not." She exaggerated chomping into a fry.

"Religious how?"

"I don't know. Weird stuff. Bible stuff."

"You just said it wasn't Christian."

"Parts of the Bible I never heard of."

"Because you're oh-so-religious?"

She considered. "You ever hear of Onan?"

"No. Who is he?"

She looked around and leaned across the table to whisper. "God of male masturbation."

"That's not real," I said.

"Men worshipping themselves? Sounds real to me." She shrugged. "She asked all this sex stuff."

"Sex stuff?"

"For an old woman, she's pretty horny." Emma raised another fry. "She asked if I was a virgin."

My face warmed.

"Which, of course," Emma said like an actress starting a soliloquy, "I am not. Far from it at this point. James DePoint, 10th grade. He's got my virginity. Maybe I can find him, see if he's been taking good care of it. Maybe I can get it back. I'd be able to wear white at my wedding."

"You're getting married?"

She laughed, too loud and forced. "Kill me, right?"

She's nervous, I thought. *Why?*

"Is this woman, like, losing it? Dementia? Alzheimer's?"

"Probably," Emma said. "Live long enough and we all get there."

4

NOW, WE WERE IN THE small librarian's office behind the circulation desk, Emma sitting on the desk, barefoot, her toes flexing along the desk's edge, and me staring disapprovingly from the doorway.

"You're talking about the same creepy old woman who asked if you were a virgin?"

"Yes. Why? Did you finally? Can I congratulate Colin?"

She was ready to leap off the desk.

"No and no."

"He's cute," she said. "Dumb too."

"Be nice."

"I am. The dumb ones make the best lovers."

"Ugh. Stop."

"Would you prefer 'sexual partner'?"

Emma arched her back, hair falling past her shoulders, and gave me the sultry come-on expression, complete with lip-tracing tongue lick, another inside joke from our giggle sessions where we embarrassed each other with staged simulations of sexual acts.

"What do I actually have to do for this woman?"

"Nothing really. Read to her. She'll love that."

"Be straight with me. What am I getting myself into?"

"She's harmless. You're going to love her."

"Right." I crossed my arms. "You know, I'm not the nursing major."

"She doesn't need a nurse. There's a schedule on the fridge for her pills. You're not giving her shots. You don't even have to bathe her. Just help her not fall down. You can do that, can't you?"

"Why're you soliciting me?"

"Soliciting? How risqué."

"Be serious."

She put on her best I'm-Being-Serious face. "You're the only one I trust."

"Why can't *you* keep doing it?"

She flexed her toes, nails fresh-painted white, and the gold rings on her big toes made clackey sounds against the desk. "Big exam coming up. Certification. Have to study. Thank you for understanding."

"I haven't agreed to anything."

"Sure, you have. You're listening to me."

"That's how people make informed decisions."

"No," she said and gave me a terribly familiar look—the one that meant she was going to get what she wanted and I damn well knew it—"saying that is how people convince themselves they've made an informed decision about something they're going to do regardless."

"You're a real bitch, you know that?"

"It's why you love me."

"What is this really about?"

"Helping an old woman."

"We've been friends forever, right?"

"Which is why you're going to help me out. You're so wonderful."

"Which is why I know you've got a secret agenda."

She put her hand on her chest. "Moi?"

"Oui."

She jumped off the desk and we were face-to-face like lovers. She gently palmed my cheek and I smelled her floral face cleanser. She'd always been a close-talker and toucher, a boundary-less woman.

"I love you so much."

"Shut up."

"You've got to do this for me."

"Tell me this isn't because you're going on one of your boy-conquering missions."

WHAT EVER HAPPENED TO JO ROSE?

She gave me another look I knew well. This one meant, *Don't ask questions you really don't want the answers to.*

Emma used boys the way boys used girls, if you know what I mean, her go-to line something like *No one thinks anything of it when a guy brags about getting another notch in his belt, but a girl who wants some dick is immediately a whore,* so I guess that was a win for feminism?

"When is it?"

"What?"

"Your exam."

"Next week."

"One week?"

"It'll be over before you know it."

"I don't trust you," I said.

"Hey," Emma said, "worst-case scenario you'll get some great ideas for stories."

"About an old woman?"

"You're always saying you want to write a novel. She'll inspire you."

"She's that interesting?"

"She'll regale you with tales of her acting glory."

"Was she actually famous?"

"She was in one movie, I think. She did a lot of local theater."

"Great."

"Babe," she said, and put both hands on my cheeks, "it's all book material. Trust me."

Was Colin watching us through the glass? Hoping we'd kiss?

I like 'em tight.

"Don't call me 'babe.'"

"This'll be good for you," she said and stepped back, hands on her hips, and gave me an up-and-down. "Miss frumpy. A sexy librarian should have a form-fitting sweater and a pencil skirt. And heels. And glasses. Didn't they teach you that in college?"

"I failed that course."

"Clearly."

"When do I start this job?"

"Tonight," she said as if that were obvious.

5

COLIN WATCHED EMMA WALK OUT of the library. He saw me and pretended something was in his eye.

"Reading anything good?" I asked.

He looked confused, an expression both cute and irritating, then glanced down at the open magazine—a bikini-clad woman leaning across the hood of a red sports car—and pushed it away like something offensive.

"What'd Emma want?"

His look was that of a little boy hopeful for a surprise gift.

"Why?"

"What?"

Was he picturing her butt? Imagining his hand on it? Imagining me and Emma together? Or God help me, a threesome?

"What?" I asked.

He started to ask the same thing again and I stopped him. "Sorry. She wants me to check on this old woman she takes care of."

"Why you?"

"Why not me?"

That cute-and-irritating look again.

I should break up with you, I thought. *Save us both the time and energy.*

He stood, the chair almost toppling over, and cupped my

shoulders. With his bright eyes and uncombed hair and letterman's jacket he might've passed for eighteen.

"What's the last book you read?" I asked. "Can you remember?"

He hesitated.

"What can I do?" he asked, not seeming hurt at all.

"Are you actually a good guy or are you a good actor?"

He had the boyish smile of a leading man, attractive and innocent with a hint of mischief.

"Emma doesn't like me, does she?"

"Why do you think that?"

"It's true, isn't it?"

"She wasn't here convincing me to break up with you."

"You want to break up?"

Yes, I thought.

No, I thought.

"Of course not," I said.

His hands traced down my arms and settled on my waist. "Dinner tonight?"

"Can't. That's why Emma was here. The old woman she checks on, she needs me to do it for the next week."

"Every night?"

"It won't be late. She's old, probably eats dinner at four and is in bed by eight."

At the word "bed," his face lit up.

"You want to come over and tuck her in?"

His right thumb found the edge of my sweater and made little swirls on my skin. I shivered. "I could come over to your place and tuck you in."

"My dad would love that."

He smelled of sandalwood and rain.

"I'll sneak in. Never know I was there."

"Mr. Smooth."

His thumb pressed against my hipbone and my breath caught. He misread that as seduction-in-action and pulled my pelvis against his so I could feel his growing interest.

A man is a little boy with adult desires.

"Let's go for a ride. Get a drink or something."

We'd probably end up at Desires, a dive bar he loved, the place stinking of mildew, the glasses chipped, and we'd park in back by the dumpster so we could have some privacy and the kissing and caressing would feel good for a while and then he'd be begging for something more and pushing my head toward it.

The woman at the other table coughed.

I gently pushed Colin back and went to the circulation desk. He followed.

"A quick drink," he said. *And a blowjob,* he no doubt added in his mind.

"I'm here until five and then I have to check on Ms. Rose."

"You shouldn't let other people make your life for you," he said.

"Make my life? I'm helping my friend."

"I'm your boyfriend."

"So?"

"So you should want to be with me."

Nothing is so easily damaged as a man's ego.

"Don't be so sensitive," I said.

Annoyance flashed in his eyes. Or maybe anger.

"She needs my help."

"I need your help, too." He glanced at his feet, playing shy.

He even sounded like a little boy, sweet, vulnerable. Was it genuine or part of his charm charade?

Did it matter?

To get what you want in a man's world, you must think like a man.

"Okay," I said and put a hand on his chest. He flexed his pecs. I pretended not to notice. "After Ms. Rose, I'll text you and maybe we can get a drink."

If I showed him the comic of Office Conan carrying off woman and donut, Colin might've recognized his own victorious grin.

I want so I take.

6

MS. ROSE LIVED IN AN old Victorian among other Victorians on Main Street. I parked my white Jetta at the curb.

Hers was one of the unrestored Victorians. Weeds sprouted through all the cracks in the stone walkway up to the paint-peeling and collapsing front steps that were gradually pulling the rest of the porch with it into the ground. The bushes were untrimmed, of course, and God knew what creatures were living in there.

The house was dark. Maybe Ms. Rose was already asleep. It was almost six, after all. Old people were early-to-bedders, weren't they?

Maybe I should leave her alone, come back tomorrow.

And what if she's dead inside? I thought. *Or worse, injured and dying?*

I got out of the car and headed up the walkway.

Warrenville is one of many towns in the Hudson Valley, a suburb of New York City, the sort of place that's good to grow up in with its parks and town parades, and the kind of place leaf-peepers clog up the roads every fall as they pick our apples and pumpkins and drink our microbrews.

In May, though, the town is quiet. The air was cool and smelled earthy-sweet. If I were a romantic, I'd say the night was perfect for giddy teens to snag a slice at F&J's or older couples to stroll to the community playhouse, perfect for a quiet kiss beneath a pale-white moon.

Something moved on the roof of the turret. *Rats,* I thought.

The house was a Queen Anne Victorian complete with castle-like tower. Shingles were missing in spots, and if I stared long enough those missing spaces almost spelled out a hidden message. *Don't enter. Not safe.* A strong wind could collapse the roof.

Not rats—

A dozen or more bats flew off the tower.

The bats zigzagged in their mad-crazy, chaotic way, so different from the gracefulness of birds.

A tower on a Victorian is called a witch's hat. Look it up if you don't believe me. Fitting then that bats would nest inside it.

Go up to the turret, sweetie, and fetch my good china, I imagined an elderly woman saying. Hunched over a cane and peering at me from behind heavy bifocals, this old woman would appear so innocent and sweet but when I went into the witch's hat I'd hear her cackling as she summoned a spell and the bats attacked en masse.

Because of course an old woman who lived in a house like this must be a witch, or at least dangerous. Perhaps this was *Hansel and Gretel,* minus Hansel, and the moment I went up to the porch the door would open and the old witch would declare, *Who's that nibbling on my house?*

My good old imagination doing what it does best—unnerving me.

Two houses down, a woman stood on the lawn watching me.

She was twenty-something and fragile-looking in a full-body nightgown that sagged on her like adult clothes on a child. But she was definitely staring right at me, yellowy porch light tinting her jaundice.

That Victorian was pink and blue, restored to its wedding-cake and gingerbread trim rococoness. It was a women's-only shelter that, if rumors were to be believed, was actually a religious cult. Back when I was in high school, everyone knew a version of a story about a woman who escaped that house and was arrested running around town naked screaming about "the dawn of the age of woman" or some such thing.

This woman staring at me was not naked or spouting crazy talk (yet), and for an escapee she seemed docile, but there was something *off* about her. Is that me making an unfair assumption? Sure, but that didn't make me wrong.

I wanted to look away and couldn't. It was as if an invisible wire connected us, one carrying an electrical charge that kept me fully focused on her.

My imagination didn't need anything more to do its thing.

This woman was in danger, a captive of religious fanatics, and the only reason she wasn't running to me, begging for my help, was because she was too scared—and maybe someone inside that house was watching her.

But what was stopping me from going to her?

I'm scared, too.

Ms. Rose's porch light came on.

The light's sickly glow hazed the porch. Half the door was thick glass. A figure moved behind it.

Ghost-like, you might say.

The other woman was gone.

Like she'd vanished.

7

I DIDN'T EVEN KNOCK. THE door swung wide and not for the first time was my imagination's conjurings proved so completely off the mark it was laughable.

Had I thought this woman would be hobbling-old, bifocaled and asking for her good china?

The woman standing inside this house was straight out of a delusion.

She stood arms spread for the kimono she wore to display an elaborate yellow-and-black butterfly pattern that included the full wingspread of her arms, long black nails spiked off her fingers, her face was slathered pancake-white, her lips a slimy somehow vile red, and ridiculous fake eyelashes swooped in dramatic wings into her thick black hair, cutting scythes on her forehead.

"*I could've been one of the greats!*"

She shouted this. Her voice echoed into her house and out behind me into the night. A stage voice. A theater voice booming to the last rows in the upper balcony.

"I was *one* of the *greats!*" she declared. "Millions of people paid good money to see me grace the stage playing all the seminal roles. And I still got it, *dahhling.*"

She dragged out that word, *darling,* and then brought her hands

17

close together in a deliberate gesture and pulled them into her face where she trailed the long nails through that thick makeup so it appeared she'd been mauled.

"Ms. Rose?"

I wasn't scared, not exactly (or perhaps "not yet" is the more fitting phrase), but I sounded plenty confused. She was screwing with me, obviously, playing up her acting persona, her Norma Desmond facade, the washed-up star trapped in self-denial and delusion.

"I need a role!" she shouted. "A person! A character! I can be anyone! Give me someone! Make it someone *delicious*, and I'll make it even tastier. Give me a role so lush and alive, and I will be its beating heart and its throbbing will to live." She stepped toward me, crossing the doorway threshold—*Who's that nibbling on my house?* I thought—and she reached for me and said, "Take my hand, *dahhhling*," dragging the word out even more this time, and I held out my hand, pure reflex, and she slithered her fingers around mine, her thumbnail piercing my palm, "and come inside. You've never had someone like me. Someone so licentiously generous. Welcome to my concupiscent *bacchanalia!*"

Part of me was certain she was insane and part of me was positive this was still a put-on and yet another part was convinced I should run for my life either way. Put-on or proof of insanity, this woman was not safe to be around.

Worst-case scenario you'll get some great ideas for stories, Emma said. *It's all book material.*

"You are Ms. Rose, yes?"

Her nail pierced harder into my palm. "Of course. Who did you think I was, Helga the Hag?"

She exaggerated an eruption of laughter and released my hand. I watched amazed as a drop of blood emerged in the middle of my palm. Her nail had actually cut me.

"You'll be okay," Ms. Rose said. She sounded completely normal. Gone was the stage voice, the exaggeration—she even looked deflated in a way, shrinking down to a normal person. "My apologies. The spirit overtakes me and I get a bit zealous in performance."

The bead of blood bloomed larger.

"But that's what the stage demands. You must be larger than life. It must seem as if the stage is too small to contain you. And then you live on in the audience's mind. There, you can live forever as a god."

"Or goddess," I said, humoring her.

"Oh, no. And please don't call me an actress. I'm an actor. And the gods"—she opened her palms and glanced skyward—"are gods."

Was this Ms. Rose being a "hoot"?

"Come in," she said. "Let's take care of that blood."

If this were a movie, the crowd might now be shouting for me to run away, no chance I should go inside that house, get out while you still can! But real life is full of such moments where cowardice shames us into bravery.

Ms. Rose was a bit much, sure, but what was there to fear? Emma had been caring for her for months. All I had to do was make sure she was fed and didn't get hurt. She was a lonely old woman. She wanted company. Someone to be her audience.

The least I could do was be kind to her.

I entered Ms. Rose's house. She shut the door behind me, and it was as if I were being sealed inside a catacomb.

8

THE HOUSE SMELLED STALE, STUFFY with dust floating in faint lamplight. The foyer carpet was worn through right where I stood. Rooms crowded with ancient furniture were to the left and right, and straight ahead a narrow hall led into the dark along an ascending staircase.

This house was too big for one person, but even from the foyer I could tell she'd made it impossible to simply yank her out. There was so much in here it was an overstocked antique store. I saw weird-looking statues and figurines, exotic (and in some cases, suggestively erotic) lamps, decorative boxes, ashtrays, a ceramic bust of Shakespeare with half its head stained an ugly rust color, stacks of old paperbacks I wanted immediately to peruse, and glass tables loaded with knickknacks and mirrors and towers of women's hats, wigs, piles of clothes, tangles of costume jewelry, and shoes, and candles, candles, candles. They were all different sizes and in assorted garish holders, and even in a baroque chandelier hanging from the ceiling, dried wax like stalactites. All unlit. Everything dust-sheathed.

"Wow," I said and apologized as if I'd said something offensive.

"Give me your hand," she said.

I offered it again and this time she held it gently. "My, I did cut you."

"Part of the performance," I said. When I tried to pull back my hand, she grabbed it tightly enough to make the moment awkward and I relented.

"Yes," she said. "You are absolutely correct."

She brought her face toward my bleeding hand, a parishioner genuflecting before a priest offering Communion, and that was almost too on the nose as I watched her lick the blood from my palm. She only used the tip of her tongue. An almost delicate act.

This is going to sound yet even weirder. Have you ever had anyone lick your palm? I don't mean a dog's slather. I mean an act soft and gentle, a lover's teasing kiss. It's surprising. And the sensation lingers.

What pain there was now tingled.

What would Colin think? He'd be disgusted, I'd bet, though who knew. Sexual desires are never as straightforward as most people wish to think. And that's coming from a virgin—or at least the virgin I was then.

"Do you think that's odd?" Ms. Rose asked.

"That you just tasted my blood? Yes."

"What if it were stigmata?"

"You mean—"

She waved it off, my question as well as her own.

"Silly Christians. A *man's* religion. Anyway, I'm thinking of adding it to something I'm working on."

"Adding?"

"Tasting the blood."

Was my blood still on her tongue? Could she taste it?

"Oh. Adding it to . . . ?"

She stepped back without bumping into anything and spread her arms as she had before, showcasing the enormous butterfly pattern.

"Isn't it gorgeous?"

"Yes."

It was too, detailed and striking. Veins webbed throughout the wings and encircled two enormous eyeballs. Patterns like that were on actual butterflies and meant to frighten away predators.

Or intimidate prey.

"Did you know there's a specimen of cannibalistic butterfly?"

"I didn't."

"You think I'm lying?"

Her stare was playfully challenging.

"No, I just never—"

"When it's a caterpillar, it feeds off toxic plants so it's unpalatable to predators, but when it becomes a butterfly it sometimes can't help but devour its own kind. It slashes with its legs and siphons out the blood. Cannibalistic vampire butterflies, isn't that something?"

Her tongue on my palm. My tingling skin.

The imaginary audience watching this movie would now be hollering, *Get out! Get out!*

Maybe, but she was an old actress (sorry, *actor*), emphasis on old, so even if she tried to attack me, I would be able to defend myself. I was in decent shape, an occasional runner who also used free weights enough I'd mastered the art of unscrewing tight jar lids. And besides, I was young.

"Emma said you're a creator."

"You mean, writer?"

"Story-maker."

"I guess."

"A teller of truthful lies."

"I like that."

Her look said she knew I would.

"Have you been published?"

"College lit mag."

"Bring me one of those stories. Tomorrow."

For whatever reason, embarrassment probably, that made me remember the book I was holding. "I brought some poetry," I said. "I could read it to you."

"Yours?"

"It's a collection. *The Best Loved Poems of*—"

Another dismissive wave and she went right into one of the living rooms or sitting rooms or whatever they might be called.

This was the perfect moment to flee. My imaginary audience might be throwing popcorn at the screen and even booing as I followed her.

The popular criticism against traditional horror fare goes like this: the people in those stories and movies don't behave the way real people would. A real person would run for their lives, but a horror story needs them to investigate the sound in the basement or run up the stairs instead of out the door or follow the creepy old lady deeper into her house.

Suspension of disbelief, we tell those head-shakers.

But listen: in those tales, dramatic irony works overtime and we readers and audience members know more than the characters. We paid to watch this horror show. We know what's coming, and then we chastise the characters for doing exactly what we paid to see them do. We set the mouse trap and then scold the mouse when the trap snaps its neck.

So here I submit the following: When you hear that noise in the basement in real life or you follow the creepy old lady into her house, do you ever actually believe you are in danger?

We can't all be characters in a horror story. Can we?

9

SHE MIGHT NOT BE A hoarder in the popular excessive way TV shows popularized but walking beyond this room meant following a serpentine trail.

The house wasn't as dilapidated as you might expect based on the exterior (though the flower-print wallpaper was peeling above the fireplace and a watermark resembling a nasty infection spread from the corner of the ceiling where the crown molding dangled loose), but it was as cramped and claustrophobic.

Thick-framed pictures crowded the walls, and the furniture in here was odd and ornate. The fabric was faded, once vibrant colors now muted, gold trim muddy-something. There were small tables and stools and strange-looking chairs that made me think of conjoined twins.

She sat in one of these and gestured to the connected seat. When I sat, we were now facing in opposite directions with a shared armrest. I kept my arms pulled in, hands on the book on my lap, my palms squeezed against the binding. Before me, heavy drapes completely obscured the tall windows.

"A Victorian conversation chair," Ms. Rose said. "A confidant chair. Sometimes a courting chair. We're close, we can touch, but there's this armrest between us."

Her fake fingernails caressed the fabric.

She's flirting with me. Or screwing with me. Or both.

She's old, I reminded myself. And she was an actress and theater people are all probably a little demented. She might be in the early stages of dementia or Alzheimer's.

This was a good deed I was doing.

But Emma was going to owe me, that was for sure.

"How did you become an actress—*actor*?" I asked.

"That's quite the personal question."

"Oh, sorry—"

"Have you ever mused that we're all actors?"

Mused. "Like we all play pretend?"

Everything about her was meant to distract, the makeup (which looked more like war paint now that she'd mauled her fingers through it) and lipstick, the eyelashes and hair, which must be a wig, the ridiculous things she said and the overdramatic flair with which she said them, but looking at her now I saw something personal, real you might say, in her gray-blue eyes and it was like walking in on someone naked.

What I saw was emotional pain.

She saw me seeing it.

"Who are you?" she asked, sounding serious as a cop.

"Oh, sorry. I'm Haley Fields. Emma must've—"

"Not what I'm asking. I know you're Haley. Emma told me. But *who* are you?"

Did she want to know if I was a virgin?

"All the world's a stage. You know who said that?"

"Shakespeare," I said. "I was an English major. Creative writing minor. Graduated a year early. Now a librarian. People might think it's boring but I really enjoy it."

Oh, God, shut up.

"Then you must know the rest of it?"

"Well, yeah, sure. All the world's—"

"All the world's a stage," she said, channeling that theater voice again but tinged with just the right amount of Elizabethan pomposity. "And all the men and women merely players; they have their exits and their entrances; and one man in his time plays many parts, his acts being seven ages. At first—"

"Ms. Rose," I said, desperate to cut her off for fear she might not only do the whole monologue but stand up and do the whole damn play. "Was that from something you were in?"

"That was Shakespeare."

"I mean when you opened the door."

"Ah, that was Helga the Hag, obviously. I'm a writer, too. A playwright. *What Ever Happened to Helga?* is an updated *Baby Jane* ripoff, of course, but I think it could be wonderful. And I think I could be wonderful in it. I might not be Bette Davis or Joan Crawford, though I might have a little Bette Davis, don't you think?"

She winked one of those swooping eyelashes.

"I'm not sure. I've never seen *Baby Jane.*"

"It's *What Ever Happened to Baby Jane?* and you must. It's your homework. I demand it."

"Oh-kay."

"I have a VHS of it around here somewhere but I really don't know. I barely watch TV. The acting today is atrocious."

VHS? I smiled despite the borderline-insanity of this situation. An old woman I was supposed to look after who had licked blood off my palm now wanted me to watch some old movie and thought I might have a way to play a VHS.

It's all book material, Emma said.

"You know the trick to good acting?" she asked.

"I've never acted."

"Sure, you have. We're all merely players, remember? One man in his time plays many parts."

"On stage, I mean."

"Acting is about belief," she said. "You must believe you are the character. It all must be true or it'll all ring falsely. And if you believe it, the audience will believe it."

"Sounds like good advice," I said.

"Do you think acting is akin to prostitution?"

What was I supposed to say to that? Was this a lead-up to the virgin question?

"Whores by another name, that's what one producer said to me. Shameless that man. But unfortunately typical. Though maybe he had a point."

"Ms. Rose, can I make you tea or get you something to eat?"

"Jo."

"Jo?"

"My name. Josephine 'Jo' Rose. Jo Rose is my stage name, which might unfortunately prove that producer's point. Who has stage names, after all? Exotic dancers. Whores by another name."

"Sure you don't want to hear a poem?" I tried.

Ms. Rose, Jo, made a loud half-sigh/half-moan and I started as if poked. "You must think I'm some deluded old woman with one-and-a-half feet in the grave and most of her brains seeping out her ears."

"Of course not."

It was warm in here, though not so warm to explain the sweat slicking my lower back.

We sat without speaking for a near minute. It was the first moment of real silence since I'd arrived. It should've been welcomed. We librarians are used to silence. As a matter of course, we relish it, love it, forever shushing even the most unoffensive chair-squeak or cough. The silence inside a library offers a communal reprieve from the noise of life, a space for reflection and thought.

But sometimes silence has its way of getting louder; it cottons up the ears and spider-walks along the skin.

It unnerves.

Your throat itches the need to cough, your feet to stamp, your hands to clap, your lungs to scream.

Then I heard something. Or thought I did. Because that's the other thing about silence—it makes you *hear* things.

Creaking sounds like you're on a boat, the type of thing we tell ourselves is the house "settling," as if the house's foundation is in constant battle with an unsteady earth. Maybe it is. Maybe we all are.

I tried hard to listen. To decipher. Wind against the windows? Those bats swarming on the roof?

It sounded like someone whispering.

I turned to Ms. Rose, trying to catch her in the act. My imagination offered me a Fuseli-*Nightmare* of a poltergeist crouched beside her, its invisible lips puppeteering hers (*and wasn't that also known as Old Hag Syndrome?*), but her lips were sealed and her head was tilted just enough to suggest she heard the sound too.

Coming from somewhere *inside* the house, upstairs I thought, someone pressed to a closed door, exhaling an incantation.

"Is someone in the house?"

Was the sound getting louder or was that a trick of the silence?

"You look a bit peaked," she said, saying it *peek-id*. "Was it the blood? If I'd known you were faint-hearted, I never would have . . ."

She didn't finish the thought but I flinched from her reach. What if she tried to cut me again? Those fake nails looked longer and sharper than before. A whispered conjuration. A blood offering.

Ridiculous.

"No one is here?"

"We are."

"Upstairs?"

She looked directly above as if she could see through the ceiling. Her wig slipped, revealing a moon crescent of scalp.

"It's a very old house."

"Settling," I said.

"Most likely, or . . ."

"Or? Or what?"

"I did have a boarder," Ms. Rose said. "Young man. Transient, I think. He kept to himself. Prurient interests, was rather distasteful, unfortunately."

"You're saying he's upstairs?"

"No reason to have boarders anymore. I have Emma. She's so wonderful. So cooperative."

Now she was staring at me. The finger-gouges she'd clawed through her makeup were jagged and more and more of it had shedded while she spoke, paint chipping off an old sculpture. I wanted it to stop flaking off and also fall off completely. I wanted her to slather whatever plaster she'd used on her face yet also scrub it all away, expose her actual skin, pale and wrinkly, and human.

"Are you frightened of me?"

My hesitation was all the confirmation she needed.

"You *should* be afraid of old women. We know things others never will. We outlive. We endure. We survive. Are we vile? Are we crazy? Or are we the truth of human experience?"

Were these more lines from her *Helga* play, or was she being serious? And if she was serious, what was I supposed to say about being scared of old women?

"Can I help you clean off the makeup?"

"Darling, you can give an old woman a facelift, but you can't give her back her youth. Once your youth is gone it's gone forever."

She patted my arm, her palm soft and fleshy, and I thought I might scream, but I managed to get a hold of myself just in time. I forced air through my teeth until my lungs were burning and then inhaled back through my clenched jaw and felt immediately better, calmer.

Dad taught me that trick when I was little and scared of thunder and fireworks and even of the house phone, which I stared at suspiciously like a bomb that might explode any moment with its high-pitched ringing shrill.

"Oh!" she said. "That's a good line. I should write that down. A perfectly Helga thing to say. Don't you think?"

"Sure."

A curl of makeup creeped off her cheek like the peel of decaying skin.

I looked at my hands instead.

What was it about this woman, this place, that was creeping me out so much? Why was I so goddamn uneasy?

"The world has been mean to you, hasn't it?"

"I don't know. I guess." Dad sitting me down, explaining how something in Mommy's brain broke.

"The world has been mean to me," Ms. Rose said. She looked around. "You must think it crazy of me to live in this house with all these things. Old and useless antiques and costumes."

I didn't know if she expected an answer so I stayed quiet.

Then she turned, faced me. "Why are you a writer?"

The question was so surprising I couldn't respond. This whole time I'd been expecting some weird sex-themed interview and I'd been on edge, which might also explain my hearing things and near panic attack, but all she wanted to know about was my writing?

"I don't know. I enjoy it?"

"Terrible answer. *Why* do you write?"

It didn't matter if I knew the first thing about being a home care aide or if I could do laundry or make tea or play pinochle; she wanted to know about me the writer.

I was a writer, novice anyway, and she was writing a play. How coincidental.

My creative writing professor said our lives are filled with coincidences, random encounters and seemingly arbitrary events, but "in our stories, some coincidences aren't coincidences at all."

Everything has a purpose.

It's all book material.

"I write because I want to give meaning to the apparently meaningless."

An answer begging for professorial approval, but Ms. Rose didn't look impressed. "You know the writer Michael Stiffe?" she asked.

"Maybe," I said. What else was a reputable librarian and writer supposed to say?

WHAT EVER HAPPENED TO JO ROSE?

"An author of little note. Something of a pervert, actually. He's a man, so no surprise there. But when asked why he's a writer, he likes to say, 'Puberty made me a writer.' An answer played for laughs, but that's what writing is."

I nodded as if I understood.

"Truthful lies." Her nails grazed my arm. I willed myself not to flinch. "Writing is telling the truth through pure fabrication."

"I think that's true," I said. I do, too.

"So, tell me: Did puberty make you a writer?"

"Sure," I said. "I guess you could say that."

Ah, finally getting to the sex stuff. I swallowed. Would she ask for specifics? When was your first period? Your first sex dream? Your first orgasm?

My throat was tight, my head beginning to cramp toward a headache.

Instead, she laughed a single note and clapped her hands together. "Excellent." Her fingers folded as if in prayer. "You're going to be perfect."

Was that more whispering I heard or just me shifting in my seat?

"Time for bed," she said in an almost completely normal voice and then yanked herself to her feet and was acting once more, arms balleting, "To bed! To bed!"

"Shakespeare," I said. "*Macbeth*."

She smiled. "See? Perfect."

I got up and followed the path out of the room.

At the staircase, she paused and pulled off her wig. Wisps of blondish-yellow-white hair made cold breath around her skull.

"Can I help at all?" I asked.

"You will. I have no doubt. And you'll help yourself, too."

"I mean with getting ready for bed."

"Of course not. I can handle myself. I'm very resourceful."

There was a small wooden box on the steps, big enough for a couple baseballs, perhaps. Dark wood and antique-looking like everything else. She picked it up and cradled it in one arm. Something was engraved on it but she covered it with her other hand before I could see.

"That's a nice box," I said, thinking I *like 'em tight*.

"It's special," Ms. Rose said. "I shouldn't leave it lying around."

Was there money in it? Valuable jewels?

In the spaces between her creaking steps up the stairs, I strained

30

to hear anything that might be a whisper. What if that transient boarder was up there, having sneaked in, and was now lying in wait to attack Ms. Rose and steal that box or whatever might be stashed in the wall behind any one of the heavy-framed pictures.

"Sure I can't accompany you?" I asked.

How funny to have been so desperate to leave and now be volunteering to stay.

"Don't forget your homework," Ms. Rose said.

"Oh, right. *Baby—What Ever Happened to Baby Jane?* Yes. If I can order from the library or stream it."

She stopped, gave me a confused look.

"Streaming," I said, "it's how most movies and shows are watched now."

Her look didn't change, but she cut me off before I could ramble on.

"Remember to bring me one of your stories. I *must* read one. One of the *published* ones, *dahhling*."

She ascended the staircase, one hand caressing the banister.

10

THE PART OF ME THAT was afraid of Ms. Rose (afraid of her the way I would be of a wild, unpredictable animal) was positive I wouldn't be able to open the door. It really would be sealed. I really *was* trapped in a catacomb.

If the knob gave even the slightest resistance, I'd be teeth-breathing again and trying not to collapse in an over-dramatic paroxysm of panic.

Ms. Rose might applaud. All the world's a stage, after all.

The door opened easily and the cool night air practically hauled me out and down the porch toward my car.

I was almost there when someone grabbed me.

It was the woman who'd been watching me. The one who'd been outside the bright-painted Victorian. The women-only cult. I'd thought she looked *off* and now, up close, I saw why.

"She's dangerous," the woman said. Her voice quavered. Her eyes jittered. And even through her squeezing fingers on my arm I felt the internal shake trembling through her, as if her own blood was whirling in a blender. "Stay away! She's bad! *Bad!*"

I pulled from her grasp, the poetry book gripped in my hand as if I might smack her with it.

She was slender, even slight, yet I sensed she could overpower me (my jar-opening strength notwithstanding), but she didn't try. She actually backed up a step. Face drawn and skeletal, nightgown wrinkling around her, she was a young woman but could've passed for forty- or even fifty-something.

"Who are you?" I sounded surprisingly composed.

She shook her head. "Not natural," she said. "No."

I slipped my free hand into my pocket. *Hit her with the book and stab her with the car key. If it comes to that.*

Yeah, right. Like I was the female John Wick.

"Go away," I said.

"She's the monster." A blue vein squiggled at her temple. "She'll make you one too!"

Another woman had come out on the front porch of the candy-colored Victorian. *That's where the witch is, in the house that actually looks like it's made of edible sweets.* This woman was stocky in jeans and a blouse and looking completely in control. She spotted us, called back inside the house, and two other women appeared, basketball-player-sized.

All three headed our way.

"You should go back," I said. "They're coming for you."

The woman glanced, saw, and then pounced—she seized both of my forearms in her clammy grip.

I didn't move. So much for hitting and stabbing.

"Ask your friend! She knows!"

She's damaged, I thought. *She doesn't know what she's saying. She's been abused.*

She let go of me and ran back across the lawn. She was barefoot. The two tall women immediately bookended her, arms interlocking behind her neck, and then the one in jeans and a blouse stopped them. She lifted a hand to the woman's face, and I clearly thought, *She's going to slap her,* but it was a caress, the way you might try to comfort a frightened child. They hugged and went inside the house.

The woman in jeans turned back to look at me, silhouetted in the open doorway.

I couldn't see her expression, couldn't be sure of anything except the gut-certainty that she was going to remember who I was and would be keeping watch.

I got in my car and went home.

11

EMMA DID NOT ANSWER HER cell or respond to any texts, which although not unusual, especially for a girl who could ignore my texts for days when she felt like it, escalated my responses rapidly from *You around?* to *I know you're not studying* to *Thanks so much for making me do your job* to *Guess you're in bitch mode now.*

No response.

Studying for her big nursing exam.

Boy conquest, more likely. Belt-notching.

Or was that me just being mean, blaming her because I was stressed and scared. Halfway home I pulled over, my heart racing so fast I had to do the breathing trick again.

But it *was* Emma's fault. *She* made me do it. If not for her, I would've spent my night reading the new Megan Abbott or Kelly Braffet or maybe writing a new story.

Emma took advantage. That was her way. She knew I would help her. That's what friends are for, right? This was no different than her begging to copy my geometry homework in high school or making me get a boy's Snapchat username. She used me.

Christ, was I really this pouty and pathetic?

Especially considering you're a virgin who's very good at saying "No."

Ha ha, real funny.

"Sorry about the messages," I said when I finally left a voicemail. "It was a strange night. All book material, right? Anyway, I guess you're studying. Call me or text." I paused and signed off our usual way, doing a pale imitation of the hillbilly voice Emma long ago mastered: "I like 'em tight."

Sitting in my car in the driveway, I managed to laugh. That made me feel better. It was going to be okay. A weird night, no question about that, but what had really happened? I spoke with a strange old woman in her decrepit house and was then accosted by another strange woman (one suffering a host of mental difficulties, I assumed) who warned me about that first one.

I wasn't ever in real danger. What was there to fear?

We call this rationalization.

I could almost hear my imaginary audience yelling at me.

This wasn't Emma's fault. She needed breaks sometimes, that's all. Call them "hiatuses," if you want, but I understood it. She seemed so cool and in control but there were plenty of long nights when I hugged her close as she cried on my shoulder.

We're all messed up.

A text arrived. Colin. *Can't wait to see u*.

Shit.

After a few false starts in which I weighed a migraine-excuse against the need-time-to-myself truth, I responded with *Still here. Could be a long night.*

Miss u, he wrote. Would it kill him to spell out the whole three-letter word?

Me too.

Want you.

Ugh. *A man is a little boy with adult desires.* Should I text him that? *Gotta go!*

He responded: *Want u BAD!*

Was I supposed to swoon at that? Not that he even knew what "swoon" meant.

I got out and then sighed against the car. I was being too hard on him. He was a good guy, always kind to me. Could I blame him for wanting some sort of physical connection?

Yes, because it's the only thing any man wants from a woman.

Could it really be that simple? When you got down to it, was every heterosexual man that stalker/rapist/murderer who likes 'em tight?

Steady, a man's voice said in my head. That voice lived in my head since I was a little girl. I brushed away the phantom touch on my leg.

Please tell me again why you don't think you need therapy?

Because nothing happened.

That isn't what you told me during our first session.

I told you the story.

You told me a story.

You're so fucking beautiful, another male voice said. This voice had been with me a long time, too, but those words were more recent and infected everything that voice said to me into something ugly.

Ripe cunt. Another male, another voice living in my mind, but I'm honestly not sure if those are the words he really said.

Please tell me again why you don't think you need therapy?

12

YES, I'M FUCKED UP. ANOTHER traumatized soul struggling through the mess of life. Maybe I don't keep my toenail clippings in mason jars in the basement or hunch over a computer for hours trying to track the infant-blood drinking cabal that's infiltrated our government, but are those examples really that far off from the pestering voices in my head or the self-tormenting thought-spirals from which I can't escape?

Everyone's got something.

You know you do.

Even if you're afraid to admit it.

13

COLIN TEXTED ME AGAIN BEFORE I got in the house.

Dont u want me? 😞

Cartoon office-Conan of the easily damaged ego.

Instead of texting the paragraph I typed out, I deleted it and sent this: 😛

He did not respond, but I bet he was reading a lot into that tongue.

I went inside and found my dad in the living room watching a John Wayne western, one of the ones where he's always killing Indigenous Americans.

"Mom know you're watching this?"

"She won't unless you tell her," he said.

"At least it's not a Clint Eastwood one," I said. "She really hates those."

Mom died when I was eight. Annie Carter Fields had been at the grocery store when she collapsed in the bread aisle after a blood vessel erupted in her brain. Dad and I never mentioned her death or the aneurysm that killed her. We always spoke of her as if she were alive. That never struck me as odd.

Dad gestured a *cheers to that* with his beer. "Join me?"

"You're trying to corrupt me," I said but dropped down on the couch across from his spot in the recliner.

"You're damn right."

Sixty-three, nearly bald, and carrying extra-weight around his middle, he looked every bit the part of late middle-age suburban dad, and when he smiled at me I saw the father who told me bedtime stories about a warrior princess named Haley the Mighty and the husband who danced Mom around the kitchen to their favorite Sinatra record.

On the TV, Wayne galloped after fleeing Indigenous Americans.

"You know what they say, Dad?"

"About?"

"It's problematic, what you're watching."

"You'd rather I watch Fox News?"

"They do have attractive women on there, Dad."

He smiled, just a little. "I've got enough women in my life, thanks."

"Oh," I said, "is Mom in the kitchen barefoot and pregnant again?"

"You're too smart for your own good," he said. "Just like your mother was."

Dad worked thirty years at the Port Authority, always wore a chambray button down, and liked to say "the world ain't what it used to be" as if he didn't have a liberal heart bleeding in his chest.

He was a great father and I loved him.

"Didn't expect you until late. You get fired?"

"Funny, no."

"How was she?"

"Strange."

"Good strange/bad strange?"

"Not sure."

Can I help at all? I'd asked Ms. Rose.

You will. I have no doubt, she said. *And you'll help yourself, too.*

"She's old," he said.

"So are you."

"Ouch."

Gunshots erupted on the TV.

Dad kept a shotgun in his closet. He was a member of the Rod & Gun Club in New Paltz, but he went there only half a dozen times a year. Still, though, it made me wonder.

"Why do you have a gun?" I asked.

"Uh-oh," he said. "It's one of those nights. What happened?"

"You don't even really use it. Why have it?"

"A man needs to be prepared for anything."

"A real man must have a gun to be prepared?"

He smiled. His single dimple showing. "You're so much like your mother. Brilliant. Tough. Beautiful."

"Thanks."

More gunshots.

"You didn't answer the question."

"Hoped you wouldn't notice."

I waited.

"I feel you staring at me," he said. "If I say, yes, a real man should know how to use a gun, does the conversation end?"

"Problematic."

"It's a problem for men to be men?"

"If being a man means killing things."

Today's man is the legacy of yesterday's brutal conquerer.

"Having a gun doesn't make me a killer, Haley."

"It makes it more likely."

He sipped his beer. "Something happen between you and Colin?"

"No," I said and he, knowing me quite well, waited. "He's fine, I guess. But he's a jock."

"I was a jock."

"You played tennis. Not the same."

"Ouch."

"We don't have much to talk about," I said.

"You don't like him, break up with him."

As if such things were so easy. Silly old man.

"I wonder sometimes if he's thinking things that are wrong."

"What are you talking about?" He put his beer down, looked at me. "He do something to you?"

Colin's thumb on my hipbone. "No, Dad. Stand down, soldier."

"Then what? Tell me."

"What if his head is filled with locker room talk? Insulting stuff about women."

"Thoughts are not actions."

"Those thoughts inform action. Boys talk about women like we're property, and society says that's what it means to be a man. You take whatever you want. Hence, toxic masculinity."

"Honey, boys who treat women that way are not anyone's example of masculinity. There's only one word for guys like that, assholes."

"Is it true boys are always thinking about sex?"

"Whoa. Sounds like entrapment. Is it finally time for the birds and bees talk?"

"Forget it."

"I'm sorry. I'll be serious." He muted the TV as another guy erupted blood. "What do you want to know?"

"Okay. What makes a man?"

"Easy," he said.

I held up a hand. "Don't say 'testicles.'"

Another smile.

"And by the way, we had the birds and the bees talk," I said. "You ruined Haley the Mighty, remember?"

It took a moment. "She fell in love."

"She put down her sword and let Prince Charming take care of her. They rode off on a horse to a magic land where they got naked."

"I really said that, did I?"

"You did your best."

Would've been easier if Mom had been alive to do it, was the unsaid part we were both thinking.

Dead people are good at filling in life's pauses.

"A man should be tough," he said. "Fair and courageous. He should defend the weak and protect the people closest to him. He shouldn't go looking for a fight but he shouldn't back down from one either."

"Are you quoting John Wayne?"

"Maybe."

"And he should save the day?"

"Nothing wrong with a man saving the day," he said. "Especially if it's John Wayne."

"You don't think I could save the day?"

"Of course you can. You're smart and brave. And one of these days, you'll let me take you shooting."

"I don't think I need a gun to save the day."

"Maybe not," he said, "but I'll tell you one thing."

"What's that?"

His one dimple pinched his beard. "Anyone ever hurts you, I'll kill the bastard."

14

I TEXTED EMMA AGAIN LATER.
Are you alive???
No response.

15

AT THE LIBRARY THE FOLLOWING day, I was reading *Slaying the Masculine*, the guide to helping women survive in a man's world but which was mostly warnings about male behavior with accompanying cartoons of Office Conan and his large-breasted female colleagues.

Nothing is so easily damaged as a man's ego . . .

Here, Conan stood dejected, head down, pouty as a little boy with the woman who just rejected him standing over him, arms somehow crossed over those breasts, her smile vindictive.

. . . but he'll hide it in a mask of rage.

Head up, face screwed into a battle-cry visage, Conan held his sword to the woman's throat, her eyes huge, and her thought bubble saying, *I better go on a date with him or he might hurt me.*

How sad it might actually be that simple.

"No boyfriend today?"

I looked up from the book I was hunched over at the Circulation Desk and saw the middle-aged woman with glasses who'd been coming for the past several days. At the table where she'd been working, the stacks of books were growing.

"Sorry to interrupt," she said. As usual, the woman's glasses nested in her thick black hair. She wore silky layers, the sort of thing a palm reader might wear in a horror movie.

"Of course not," I said. "How can I help you?"

Although most days at the library were quiet (both in the *shh*-finger-on-lips way and in the not-much-to-do way), every so often someone would come up to the desk and ask for help crafting a résumé or studying for a realtor's exam or researching ancient Mesopotamia or, in one case, the breeding habits of piranhas.

I'm always happy to help, as long as real piranhas aren't involved. Books, after all, are safer.

"Have you heard about The Gelder?" the woman asked.

"Isn't that someone who neuters horses?"

The woman smiled. It was almost sly. "Someone's been assaulting men—and neutering them."

"You mean?"

"Yeah."

"Really?" My own enthusiasm surprised me.

"He's got six or seven now, I think."

"Whoa. Where is this?"

"Not too far," she said with that same almost-cunning grin. "Rochester area."

"Oh." I'd gone to college out there. So had Emma. I went to Geneseo, she to Binghamton. "Whoever it is, is actually . . ." I couldn't finish.

"Cutting off their balls, yes."

"Shit." Someone was castrating men. Attacking them and severing their balls. It made me both nauseated and exhilarated. Is that awful to admit? Emma wouldn't think so. She'd love this, if she ever responded to my texts.

"You think you could help me research it?"

"I can try."

She leaned toward me, whispered, "Between us, I hope it's a woman doing it and she gets at least a few more before she's caught." She saw my uncertainty but instead of backing off she doubled down: "Men have done a lot worse and they've been doing it since the beginning."

"I guess you're right."

"It's custom in some countries to mutilate girls' genitals when they hit puberty. But of course we're not allowed to criticize them for it. Have to respect every culture even if it's rooted in centuries of female degradation. Isn't that interesting?"

"Or terrifying," I said.

"Correct. I'm Gabi, by the way. Gabi Esposito."

"Haley Fields." I gestured to her stacks of books. "Is that about this?"

"Doctoral dissertation. Gender studies."

"What's your thesis?"

She breathed in. "The patriarchal corruption of naturally intended matriarchal dominance through systematic societal, cultural, religious, and anthropologically embedded sexism, misogyny, and violence."

"Impressive," I said and slid *Slaying the Masculine* toward her. "You might like this."

"Oh?"

"Today's man is the legacy of yesterday's brutal conquerer," I said.

"Now you're speaking my language."

16

IT DIDN'T TAKE LONG TO uncover the basics.

Since February, seven men from Binghamton to Rochester had become victims of The Gelder.

The first was a middle-aged man who was found beaten unconscious in an empty parking lot with his testicles removed.

From an article titled "Man Assaulted, Gelded," which was after the third attack, the Sheriff of Livingston County said, "The extent of the sexual mutilation is extreme. The victim's scrotum was completely severed and is gone. This is the work of a very, very sick individual, and we will bring that individual to justice."

From what I could find, there were no leads, no witnesses other than a man who may or may not have been drunk when he "saw a group of four people in all black go at this guy, beat him, and then take him away." That was outside a sports bar and the witness neglected to report it for nearly a full day so his testimony might not be the most reliable.

But things did get even more interesting when I found the following article: "Gelded Man Is Sexual Predator."

The second victim was a registered sex offender. He was convicted of "sexual misconduct with a minor."

The fifth victim was an "accused sexual stalker" who'd been

charged with "sexual malfeasance" and "sexual impropriety" as well as "sexual assault," but whose case ended in a mistrial because of a "prosecutorial procedural error."

"And now he's got no balls," Gabi said. "Vigilante justice."

"Might be a little morbid for a PhD," I said.

Gabi touched the glasses on her head as if to use them but simply readjusted them. "Depends if men are reading my thesis," she said.

She returned to her table of stacked books, her layers clinging and peeling as she moved, and I thought again of how she resembled a fortune-teller in a movie.

Then I returned to The Gelder.

17

CUTTING OFF THEIR BALLS.

It was one of the most awful things I'd ever heard and yet as I read and reread the details some internal flame of interest flickered brighter and brighter.

These men were sexual predators. I found four more of the "gelded" who had records of sex crimes. One was a serial flasher terrorizing public playgrounds and found guilty of "indecent fondling." One was a molester. One was a rapist who'd served three years.

Only one of the victims, a 26-year-old named Dominic Evans who was arrested twice for "forced sexual congress" was never formally charged. The reporter for that article listed "an anonymous source" as the credit for that information.

New York State maintains a Sex Offender Registry of low to high-risk offenders, which includes in most cases the offenders' addresses. If that wasn't enough, there were also people who kept updated Good Samaritan and Keep Our Kids Safe lists that offered even more information—pictures (most of these cellphone shots taken at a distance), summary of crimes, jobs, previous addresses, known acquaintances, and more.

Whoever The Gelder was, at least based on what I could discover, they were targeting men who deserved it.

Should I admit that? Those men might not be guilty. That was a possibility, yet even if they technically were "not guilty," that didn't make them "innocent."

That is what we call slippery moral ground. Then again, what woman ever deserved anything a man did to hurt her?

So, yeah, that flickering flame quickly became a fire.

I told you everybody's fucked up.

Sick as it is to admit, it was thrilling, and that wasn't even the sickest part.

In every case, the castrated male's injury was treated (in one case cauterized, the others bandaged) so the victim wouldn't bleed out.

It wasn't about killing these men. It was about removing their manhood. Literally.

Which brought up the obvious question beyond who was doing this.

The removed scrotums from all seven men were missing.

What was the attacker doing with them?

18

I TEXTED EMMA: *HOW'S THE* box? Is it tight?

No response.

PART TWO:
NIGHT OF
THREE STORIES

19

NO STRANGE CULT WOMAN WATCHED me this time when I returned to Ms. Rose's. There were no bats, either. Nor was she in costume.

Ms. Rose, in blouse and slacks, opened the door, saw the magazine in my hand, and snatched it before I could say anything.

I followed her inside.

Closing the door behind me, I was struck by the amusing realization that just yesterday I'd been almost terrified I'd never escape this house and now here I was willingly closing myself inside it. Ms. Rose had not only cut me yesterday, she had *tasted* my blood, licked it off my palm. But was that really such a big deal?

Someone was turning sexual predators into eunuchs. It was men who should be afraid, not me, and certainly not of an old woman whose real crime was self-aggrandizing delusion.

That's what I thought then anyway.

20

WE SAT IN THE SAME serpent-curled conversation chair. Two cups of tea waited on side tables. Ms. Rose sipped hers but mine looked like dirty water so I thanked her and didn't drink it. Just as well, the teacup looked a hundred years old, aged and unwashed.

The room smelled mustier than it had yesterday, the air thick with it. The heavy-framed paintings tilted more steeply off the walls, looming over me, as if the picture of faded gray fruit or the mortician-dressed man with the pale hands or the matronly woman with piercing eyes or the cherub-baby on what looked like a drugged-donkey were each trying to get a better look at me.

Like I'm cornered prey.

Ms. Rose was flipping through the magazine. She'd passed my story several times already. "I can't find it. Where is it?"

"Page twelve," I said.

She riffled pages, found it. I thought she might ask me to read it to her, but after a moment she said instead, "Ah, I see. How terrible."

No writer wants to hear someone currently reading their work remark, "How terrible," unless the reader is commenting on the events as opposed to the writing.

What happens in the story is terrible but she'd only just started reading. I didn't think the story events were that obvious.

Her hand settled on my arm. The fake nails were gone. Her skin was warm.

She looked at me. The heavy pancake makeup was gone, too, replaced with light blush and coloring. She could've been anyone's innocuous grandma. Maybe she was.

"You were molested," she said. "I'm sorry."

Her expression was pure kindness and I was struck silent. She turned back around and continued reading.

21

"Reflexes"
By Haley Fields
Originally published in The Peripatetic Observer, *Issue 45, Fall 2019.*

YOU'VE ALWAYS HAD GOOD REFLEXES. You're naturally athletic. Dad says "Hey, Princess," and the moment you turn, a tennis ball is flying at your head. You catch it. Every time. Mom doesn't care for the throw-things-at-my-little-angel routine, but you love it. You never miss. It's pure reflex.

Your gym teacher throughout elementary school is Mr. Reynolds, a tall, thin man who always wears red shorts and a white polo regardless of the weather and has a silver whistle on a lanyard around his neck. Mr. Reynolds notices your "fluid speed," "intuitive grace," and, of course, "whip-like reflexes," and he takes it upon himself to work with you three times a week during recess to develop your "athletic potential."

You could be a great athlete someday.

Mr. Reynolds teaches you softball and tennis and also strength-training exercises and tumbling and handsprings and gradually works you into more and more complicated things like the uneven bars and the pommel horse. You take to every challenge as though you have been designed to master it.

"A gifted gymnast," he says. "Great instincts."

When you scissor your way back and forth faster and faster on the pommel horse, kicking your legs higher and higher with each pass, and then do a handstand and even manage a decent dismount, Mr. Reynolds gives you a big hug.

He pulls you against his chest. Your face rubs into the black curls of hair poking from the V in his polo. He smells of sweat.

Several weeks, and many, many more tight hugs later, you are running through your usual warm-up exercises when you get flat on the gym mat, arms at your sides, palms down, and Mr. Reynolds places a red cloth that might be an identical pair of his gym shorts between your bare feet.

"Squeeze the cloth between your feet," he says through the whistle in his mouth, "and raise your legs over your head."

Mr. Reynolds is kneeling beside you, smiling around the whistle in a weird way. You are almost ten and adults are constantly surprising you with the odd things they say and the strange faces they make.

Mr. Reynolds places his hand on the underside of your exposed thigh. It is warm and moist like the washcloth Mom used to clean your face in the tub when you were little.

"Steady," Mr. Reynolds says. "Steady."

You clench your stomach muscles and push off your hands to move your legs farther past your head. The laughter of kids playing tag outside this empty gym sounds far away.

"Very good." His voice deepens like he has something stuck in his throat and the whistle falls. His saliva gleams on it. You smell the sharp odor of his sweat, acrid and pungent like when the kitchen garbage needs to be taken out. His hand slides down your thigh.

Your muscles, seemingly all of them and all at once, shake like the foundation of a building during an earthquake.

"Steady." His hand slips lower and his smile stretches. The laughter of the kids outside echoes all around, mocking.

His breath huffs bull-like through his nose.

The whistle dangles in your face.

You squint into the spaceship lights, Mr. Reynolds shadowed above you, yet you see the way his mouth spreads like Play-Doh.

"Steady," he says.

You dare to look at him. His brown eyes are black. His teeth look sharp.

His hand slides farther, fingertips at the curve of your butt and—and you don't hesitate, don't fret over consequences, don't have to use your brain at all because your body reacts in one, quick reflex.

You push off your hands as hard as you can and tumble feet over head. Mr. Reynolds' hand catches in the crook of your knee and holds you a moment but your legs scissor back and forth to thwack him in the face and throat.

He is facedown on the mat choking for air when you run out of the gym and back to your classroom. Your bare feet make loud smacking sounds on the cold floor.

When your parents ask what happened the expressions on their faces say things have changed, that you are no longer Daddy's princess or Mommy's little angel, making accusations about such a respected man, and so you don't think twice. You lie. It's pure reflex.

"It was a mistake," you say.

Is it also a mistake thirty years later when your foot slams on the gas pedal instead of the brake? It might not have mattered if it had been a deer running across the road, but it isn't any unlucky animal: it's a person.

"Just standing there," you whisper to yourself.

Except, you'd swerved the tiniest bit. Swerved *toward* the man.

"Steady."

Through the rearview mirror, you see the man is on the street, facedown, arms tucked under his chest, legs wrapped around each other. His mail flutters to the ground around him.

You get out of the car.

This back road that you take every day to the Gymnastics Center where you teach little kids how to tumble, do a bird's nest, a beam pass, and every other damn thing, is one of those roads Norman Rockwell might have painted when the trees are full bloom or shedding their orange and red leaves in gusts of October wind.

On this cold day, however, the bare trees lining the road are gnarled skeletons bending down for a closer look at this country-road tragedy.

The man in the street is wearing red shorts and a white polo. His face is flat against the concrete, pressed into it like the road is made of dough. Not the road, of course; it is the man's face that has turned to mush. Swirls of blood circle the man's shirt like the lines on a candy cane and an elongated splotch of blood fans out from his crushed head.

You walk closer.

A dog is barking.

A silver whistle on a lanyard lies in a streak of blood.

One of his hands pokes out from under him, palm flat as though he had tried to brace himself or his final act was reaching for that whistle. A chill starts on the back of your thigh and worms its way up.

The man's house, opposite from his mailbox, stands quiet and frost-covered.

You'd been speeding down this road as usual—a road your parents took to bring you to private gymnastics lessons in the basement of this very house—and reaching into your bag for a cigarette to ease your hangover, and when you glanced up, there he was in red shorts with a white polo and a silver whistle around his neck just standing in the middle of the road as though your barreling car was exactly what he had been waiting for.

Or what you had been hoping for all these years.

Steady.

After everything you endured in Mr. Reynolds' basement, it's a wonder you kept with gymnastics.

Booze and Adderall helped. Still do.

Steady.

And your reflexes that never failed you in thirty-eight years drove your foot flat-down on the gas. The car thumped into and over him like a devouring beast. Your bag belched its contents. The Marlboros landed on the floor. Your triple shot espresso splashed everywhere.

You step closer. A dead man in gym shorts and a polo with a whistle.

Your eyes trail up to the man's mailbox. Faded stenciled letters on the side of it: Reynolds.

You did it. You finally got him.

A laugh hiccups free.

Sometimes we do things because the seed of it is buried in the muddy subconscious where childhood traumas forever sprout poisoned roots.

A man driving an SUV calls the police, and you ask him if he believes in karma. "Does everyone eventually get what's coming to them?"

"What do you mean?"

You are laughing again but it dies when the red gym shorts turn into brown pants and the polo into a button-down and the lanyard is a leash for the yapping dog you didn't hit.

It's not Mr. Reynolds. Of course not. He retired, moved away. You know this.

Sometimes we do things because we can't stop ourselves. It's instinct.

Later, a cop asks you what happened.

You don't have to think.

"He ran out in front of me," you say. "There was nothing I could do."

It's pure reflex.

22

MS. ROSE NODDED A FEW times while reading but made no more comments until she'd finished it and closed the magazine on her lap.

"I wasn't molested," I said. "It's just a story."

"And what *are* stories?" Ms. Rose asked without looking at me.

"Works of imagination," I said.

"Truthful lies, darling."

"No," I said, my own reflex. Stubbornness, perhaps. Denial, maybe.

Ms. Rose took a breath and sat taller. She was staring straight ahead, though, through the doorway that led into another room crowded with old furniture and heavy paintings.

"I was one of the most renowned actors to ever play Lady Macbeth. Did Emma tell you that?"

"I don't . . . Maybe," I said.

"And maybe not. I played Lady Macbeth for twelve years in a community theater production. It was my performance that kept the show returning every year. It won awards. *I* won awards. I was amazing. I was recruited to perform for an off-off Broadway production in 1990. Three weeks, twenty-seven performances. 'Stunningly vivid, appealing, and terrifying.' That's what *The New York Times* said about me.

"Wow," I said but couldn't help thinking, *Have to double-check that.*

"I would've preferred to be Macbeth," Ms. Rose said. "Lady Macbeth's sad ending is unfortunate and forced. Typical arc for a female written by a male. You go crazy with guilt and kill yourself or you're saved by some white knight. Shakespeare could write, but he was still a man and so his female characters are idiots, tyrants, or whores. They either kill themselves or get forgotten."

"I hadn't really thought about it that way before." In fact, one of my college courses had been Shakespeare the Feminist.

"Men can't write women. Not even Shakespeare."

"My college professors might want to argue with you on that point, Ms. Rose."

"Male professors?"

"Yes, but—"

"Screw 'em! All men do is look out for each other's dicks."

My hand wasn't quick enough to stifle my laughter.

She glanced at me, smiling. "And call me Jo."

For the second time since arriving I was struck by my complete lack of unease. Yesterday I'd been so anxious I saw this woman as a horror-movie trope. Now, though, I found her charming, even endearing. The grandmother I never knew.

"There was a Hollywood producer who hired me to play Lady Macbeth in a filmed sequel."

"Sequel?"

"I was to be the star. *Blood Will Have Blood: Lady Macbeth's Revenge.* Silly as it sounds, the script wasn't bad. Shakespeare doesn't even care enough to have Lady Macbeth die on stage. Her death is announced—'The queen, my lord, is dead.'—and then Macbeth gives his crybaby 'Tomorrow' soliloquy. Woe is me, life is so hard. Most of the movies show Lady Macbeth's body, but what if she faked her death? Faked it and fled?"

"Then she goes around killing men?"

"She gets them all—Malcolm, Donalbain, and Macduff."

"Let me guess," I said, "she works with the witches."

"Of course."

"I guess I could see that. Was it ever filmed?"

"Funding collapsed before we could record any of it."

"That's too bad."

I meant it too. Though such a movie would probably devolve into a blood-drenched slasher with Lady Macbeth as the avenging monster concocting creative kills for each male victim, it would certainly be more interesting than Mr. *I like 'em tight* hillbilly terrorizing girls in the woods.

"He raped me," Jo said. "Mr. Hollywood producer."

I was too stunned to say anything. Not that I was shocked by the fact of it happening, not at all, but by the openness with which she so bluntly shared it.

"I should've known," she said. "How often do we women say *that* to ourselves. But I was blinded by the opportunity he was giving me, my head filling with images of seeing myself on the silver screen, of autographing headshots, accepting awards."

She laughed again, a self-mocking chuckle.

"I never would've thought. I was over forty, and men are so predictable with their tastes for young flesh."

Young flesh, I thought and almost gagged.

"But I was a very striking beauty," she said. "Well into my sixties. It's unfortunate what your seventies do to you."

"You look wonderful," I said.

She ignored my compliment, thinking about something.

"He believed acting was akin to prostitution."

"Whores by another name," I said.

"Exactly. You remembered. Why don't we ever believe men when they talk that way? They're practically confessing and we dismiss it. We make excuses for men so they don't even have to."

"Locker room talk," I said.

"Yes. Boys will be boys, after all. And rapists, too."

When she touched my arm this time, I didn't suffer some irrational panic attack as I had yesterday. Her touch didn't make my skin creep or my lungs constrict. In fact, her touch was comforting.

Her eyes found mine.

"I didn't even realize what was happening until it was happening. I came up in an age when men were very handsy. Always touching your lower back or your shoulder or your leg. They flirted and expected you to flirt back, whether you were interested or not. It was really the easiest way to get what you wanted. Make the man think he had a chance with you and everything went more smoothly. What's a little harmless petting, anyway?"

She wasn't crying, her eyes weren't even glazing, but my own began to sting. Here was a woman in her seventies who had to grow up in a time when it wasn't only accepted that men treated women like personal playthings but encouraged.

"Even when he kept going, I didn't think he'd *keep* going. But he did. I protested. But I didn't fight. I'm ashamed to admit that. I told myself this was a small sacrifice. Let this man have what he wanted and I could be in a movie."

She didn't look away, didn't even blink. Emma would've called it the Lecter-stare and quoted Anthony Hopkins saying he once ate a man's liver with some fava beans and a nice Chianti. She'd say the line with a perfect sociopathic emotionlessness and then lean toward me and make a wet slurping sound through her teeth. I'd push her away saying she was disgusting. Then we'd be laughing.

There was nothing funny about this moment, and thinking of Emma only made me angry at her. Why hadn't she texted me back? Why had she abandoned this old woman who needed someone to listen to her?

"So," she said, "he got what he wanted and I got nothing. That pretty much explains sexual politics, doesn't it?"

"Where's he now?" *Maybe The Gelder could get him,* I thought.

"Dead, fifteen years. Colon cancer. Shame it wasn't testicular."

She stood and I used the moment to blot my eyes.

"Let's get something to eat," Jo said. "Something sweet."

Maybe she meant for us to go somewhere, the diner, or Dunkin', but she walked out of the room toward the kitchen.

I got up and followed, but I paused, turned back to the room. It felt like someone was watching me. Thick drapes covered the windows. Dust swirled slowly above the lamps. The paintings, though, they crowded closer, macabre faces and sharp eyes and creepy cherub babies, watching, silent as mute witnesses.

23

IN THE KITCHEN, THE WALLPAPER was faded and peeling in places, the cabinets were dust-sticky, and the appliances looked almost as old as the furniture we'd been sitting on, but unlike the other rooms this one felt homey, almost cozy. An ornate cuckoo clock hung on the wall. It was wood-carved with pinecone weights but it appeared broken.

Beneath it was the basement door.

What was down there? More antiques? Buried secrets?

Another door led to the outside. A glazed window in it looked out at the neighbor's property. That house was dark. The one beyond that, though, pooled light across the grass.

The women's cult. What were they up to this evening? Cultish things? Silly to think, but—

Stay away! She's had! Bad!

Jo started making tea (*she's going to poison it or drug it to screw with my head*), but once I offered to help she handed over the copper teakettle.

I expected crumbly stale scones or an expired box of Entenmann's coffee cake. Instead, she scooped chocolate peanut butter ice cream into fluted sundae dishes and even topped them with whip cream and a cherry.

It was sweet and delicious. (*Unless it's poisoned . . .*) The cold made me shiver.

"You know what a lifetime of acting has taught me?" Jo ate her ice cream slowly, carefully. "You must let the fiction go. Let it drop into a deep, dark hole. Who are you really? What is your truth? That is what you need to bring into the light. The truth you experienced."

"That makes sense," I said.

"It's more than that. Acting is escape, of course. I'm not so in denial I can't see that for what it is, yet it's no more an escape than religion. Do you know what religion *is*?"

Weird stuff, Emma said. *Bible stuff.*

"Collective delusion," Jo said. "Do you believe in God?"

"I . . . I'm not sure."

"Because you're a smart woman. The smarter people get, the less they believe in the ridiculous. With some exceptions. Men, for example."

"Men just stay stupid?"

She smiled around a spoon of ice cream and ate it.

"Boys never outgrow their pride. It only gets bigger. Hurt a 35-year-old man's pride and he'll lash out same as he would at 15. He'll call you a whore."

Nothing is so easily damaged as a man's ego, but he'll hide it in a mask of rage.

Maybe I could read passages of that workplace Conan book to Ms. Rose.

"Men never give up their gods. Never." She leveled her gaze at me, Lecter-stare again. "Men have many gods—of violence, of war, of sex, of rape, of molestation, of masturbation." She hacked a mocking laugh. "The god Onan. It's a real thing. Well, real in that there are men who get together and worship with their hands, if you know what I mean."

"Emma might've mentioned it before. Men actually get together and . . ."

"And wank themselves. Oh, yes, indeed."

The ice cream melting on my tongue made me want to spit it out. "Isn't that disgusting?"

"Men are disgusting."

"Not all men."

"Yes, dear. *All* men. They are born slaves to selfish idiot gods. We mustn't let the gods men worship be our gods as well. Or even our devils. We don't need such things."

"Sounds like a screwed-up system."

"Yes, indeed, dear."

She slurped ice cream off her spoon. Dribbles spotted her blouse.

I heard something then. Soft like a breeze slipping around the house, but definitely coming from inside. A shifting, as slight as sheets sliding on a bed. From right above us. Yesterday, I'd sworn it was a whispering susurration. I'd asked if anyone else was in the house. And she'd said . . . ?

She's bad. Bad! She's a monster. She'll make you one too!

From my seat, I saw out the window into the night. Women were in the backyard behind the cult house. A circle of them. Holding hands haloed in flood light. What were they doing?

Cultish things.

"Mice, I'm afraid. Rats in the walls!"

She blurted this in grand dramatic style and I was so surprised my heart trampolined into my throat.

"I'm sorry. Didn't mean to startle you."

"It's okay. Mice?"

"An old house. Lots of the places for them to hide."

I heard it again. It was whispering. Someone speaking, face pressed to the floor, speaking to me directly overhead.

She'd had a boarder once. What had she said about him? *Rather distasteful* was he?

"No one is upstairs?" I asked.

"Mice. More ice cream?"

"No, thank you." Outside, the women were walking in their linked circle. Maybe they were chanting. Maybe that was the sound.

The Weird Sisters, hand in hand, thus do go about, about.

"You're looking peaked again."

"Nothing. Shakespeare, actually."

"The raven himself is hoarse?"

"Maybe," I said.

"You were molested," she said licking the last off her spoon. "You don't need to share your trauma with me. I don't need the facts. The truth is clear as day in every word of your story."

"I . . ."

"It's okay," she said and dropped the spoon in the dish. It clattered loudly. "Whoever it was that hurt you as a child was worshipping his own god. But you don't need a god. You need only yourself." She used a cloth napkin to blot at the spots on her blouse. "You're a virgin?"

I might've laughed. Here it was, finally, the question Emma said would come eventually, one I'd dreaded because it was so personal and inappropriate for someone to ask, a question that was automatically a judgment and whose answer or even *un*answer reddened my cheeks and cottoned my mouth.

Except after what she'd shared, none of that seemed to matter.

"Yes," I said. "My choice."

"As it should be."

"Emma thinks it's silly. I should get it over with. I'm making it out to be too big a deal."

"It *is* a big deal. Once a man sticks his dick inside a woman, it's all he ever wants. All he ever thinks about. It's the single driving force behind everything he does. I do mean everything. But man is not monogamous. He has one woman, he wants another. He beds one, he longs to bed a different one. We're playthings for them."

"A man is a little boy with adult desires," I said.

"How true. If I'd ever had a child," Jo said, "I'd have wanted her to be like you."

"Why's that?" My spoon scraped at the last melting bits of ice cream.

"Because you're braver than I ever was."

Is it pathetic to admit my eyes stung and I pretended to eat more ice cream so I could bite on the spoon?

"You have more stories." It wasn't a question. "I'd like to read another."

"Oh, okay, I can bring—"

Shaking her head, and saying, "Can't you get it on your phone? I'd like to read it right now. I'd like you to read it to me."

"I guess, I—"

I ran for the sink, my chair toppling, and made it in time for blackish slimy bile to splash from my mouth. My stomach clenched, my body arched. I gripped the counter. More fluid splashed, dark like I'd been eating ink. *Or blood,* I thought. I retched. Mushy clumps splatted. The smell wafted back into my face, humid and stagnant like swamp water.

I gagged another spasm and I was spitting the last of it. What I hoped was the last of it.

I'd never puked like that before, feeling fine one breath and then vomiting the next.

Poison in the ice cream.

Trying not to breathe in the stink, I peered closer at my puke. What were those indistinguishable glops? Was something *in* that ice cream?

One of them almost looked like a slug. Jesus, it really looked—

It twitched and I flinched back and might've screamed but Ms. Rose was right beside me, one hand at my back and the other smacking the water on, full blast hot, swirling the mess down the drain.

"What was that?" I asked.

"A good purge is good for the soul," she said. "You must feel better."

I hesitated. I did feel better. I really did.

Clear-headed, calm.

"Actually, yes, I do."

"Another story?" she asked.

24

SHE WAS RIGHT, OF COURSE. I was molested.

I was not a gymnast, not terribly (or even slightly) athletic, didn't have good physical reflexes, was the girl who according to a snotty kid in gym class threw a ball worse than a girl, but "Reflexes" was about me.

The girl in it was my stand-in. I'd deny it, and did several times after Emma read the story and asked me straight out and my father read it and couldn't erase the pitying look on his face even as he couldn't bring himself to ask if his little girl had been molested so long ago.

The gym teacher was actually a long-term gym sub named Mr. Sams. He did not say I was a natural athlete. Far from. I had "undeveloped" hand-eye coordination, and essentially no kinesthetic ability. Or to put it the way Mr. Sam's did, I had "not one athletic bone in [my] body."

"You're really behind all the other kids," he told me. "Especially for a ten-year-old." He was standing over me. Gym class had ended, the kids filing out into the hallway, a stray basketball bouncing across the floor. "But I can help you. Do you want me to help you?"

I never went to his basement for gymnastic lessons, I don't take Adderall or drink much, I'm not even on antidepressants, and I've never run anyone over, but something did happen to me.

Mr. Sams pulled me from class three times a week to work on my coordination. Throwing a tennis ball, dribbling a basketball, kicking a playground ball.

Every session was a victory, he said, and every victory deserved a hug.

The hugs got longer and tighter. He wore polos and red shorts like the Mr. Reynolds in my story and his chest hair rubbed against my face as it does against the girl's. He always smelled like milk that had gone bad.

As the hugs got longer, his hands no longer stayed on my back. They roamed.

The first time his hand touched my butt, I couldn't breathe, literally, and Mr. Sams brought me to the nurse.

Each time he'd show up at the classroom door for our sessions, my chest would get tight and my breath would sound like air whistled across an open bottle.

One day several weeks after this had been going on, Dad wanted to play catch and the moment I saw the ball in his hand I stopped breathing. That's when he taught me the force-air-through-your-teeth technique.

"What was that about?" he asked.

"I don't know," I said. Dad had no idea about Mr. Sams, the private lessons.

"Were you thinking about Mom?"

I nodded because it was an easy answer and it ended the conversation and I could cry and felt a little better.

One day, Mr. Sams wanted to teach me to do a handstand. "Most girls do them naturally," he said. "I'll help you."

When my shirt fell to my chin, his hands cupped either side of my chest. His skin was so warm. I couldn't breathe. I was shaking. "Steady," he said. "Steady." He sounded short of breath but with excitement, a kid just before he opens all his Christmas presents.

He eased me onto the mat. It was sticky plastic. He didn't take his hands from me, staring at me in a way I couldn't understand but which was terrifying. Then his hands moved to other places, and I should've screamed. I should've kicked him and run away.

I should've been brave.

The regular gym teacher returned the next week and Mr. Sams went away. Wasn't fired. Wasn't arrested. Last I heard, he retired upstate somewhere.

I should've done something, told someone, stood up for myself, but I was a little kid, a weakling who saw danger everywhere, even in confessing that something bad had happened to me.

In my story, though, I could stop Mr. Sams. Stop those roaming hands.

That's something writing can do.

We all know writing is a way to process pain, but it's also a way to create alternate pathways of our own lives, past, present, and future.

Fiction is better than autobiography or even memoir because fiction isn't imprisoned by fact; it is freed by truth.

And possibility.

So, I read Ms. Rose another one of my stories. This one's true too, all except for the ending. My character does what I couldn't. My characters are so much braver than I am.

"It's titled 'Graduation Party,'" I said.

Ms. Rose gave me her full attention there in the kitchen with the night darkening around us, women chanting or praying or whatever they were doing outside, and something above our heads either scurrying around or whispering desperately to be heard.

25

"Graduation Party"
By Haley Fields
Originally published in Tabelations, *July 2020*

HE CORNERS YOU IN THE kitchen, one hand on the counter, the other on the butcher-block island so you're trapped by the fridge, the cold pluming out over your body like something from a beer ad.

You don't see him, or at least don't acknowledge him, until you shut the door and turn, bottle of spiked lemonade in hand.

"Getting that for someone?" he asks.

The bottle is already sweating, water beads slicking your slender fingers, the nails painted school-color blue-and-gold.

"Yeah," you say, "my future self who's over twenty-one, come to party, and thirsty as hell."

"You've always been the witty one," he says.

"Learned it from you, Uncle Mike." You unscrew the bottle top and take a quick swig.

He watches you swallow. Watches a drop of lemonade fall from your lips.

He isn't really your uncle, but he's been Dad's friend since forever and in the decade since Mom died he became part of every birthday party, holiday celebration, Sunday suppers, and almost daily visits.

"Figured you'd put on your bathing suit by now. Hot enough," he says.

"Yeah, maybe," you say and steal another sip.

"Were you wearing that during graduation?"

His eyes take in your shirt that plunges low and cuts short of your bellybutton piercing, and the pockets of your jean shorts that dangle past the hem along your thighs where your only visible tattoo stretches thorny rose stems around a human skull. Your gymnast legs end in bare feet, nails painted to match your fingers, silver rings around the big toes.

"When your father and I graduated, we wore our skivvies under our gowns and that's it." He smirks as if his young self had been so bold and charming.

"Cool," you say. You want to get past him but haven't committed to trying yet. You take another sip.

"Some tattoo."

"Thanks."

"I thought you had to be eighteen to get one."

You shrug, sip more. It tastes metal-y. Uncle Mike is right, but Cory at Fresh Ink is cool and hooked you up anyway. Hooked you up with good weed too.

You stare past him at the wide kitchen and the expansive living room beyond.

"Excited for college?" he asks.

"I guess."

"You going to cheerlead?"

You tilt your head as if wondering something.

Are you thinking of all the football games he'd attended, always standing by the fence so he could watch the long-leg kicks and flapping skirts?

"Just gymnastics," you say.

"You okay?"

"Yeah, fine." Your voice tight.

"You look nervous."

"Party jitters. Is there enough food? Is the music good? You know."

You finally make a move to get past him, leaning forward and as if intending to duck under his right arm, a move you've done hundreds of times as a child, but you aren't so small and nimble anymore.

He catches your elbow. Squeezes.

He looks down into your eyes. "I want to ask you something."

You make as if to drink, but the bottle stops short of your parted lips.

"Sure you're okay?"

Outside, the thrumming hip-hop beat cuts off and in the immediate silence you try to pull from his grip, almost playfully, but he doesn't let go. People are laughing out on the deck and the young kids are splashing in the pool. Everyone is outside except for you and Uncle Mike.

"Did you have another question?"

That smirk again. His hand drops from elbow to waist, thumb on the bare flesh of your hipbone. It isn't fear so much on your face as uncertainty.

"I want to offer you something," he says. "No strings attached."

The grin, though, says there will be all kinds of strings.

"Yeah?" you say with teenager attitude. Your expression hardens, going all stone-faced bitchy as you did when your boyfriend Aiden tried to get in your pants, but Uncle Mike sees through it to the easy smiles and playful flirtations of the last several years.

The music outside blares back on—fast-paced Elvis Costello.

"Ugh," you say and roll your eyes. "Somebody let Dad hook up his iPhone. I better save the day."

With that, you try again to get past him and then somebody is in the hall talking and heading this way and that will put an end to this weird moment that's a bit too much like something that happened to you in elementary school.

Except he can't let this moment go, has spent far too much time thinking about it and finally committed himself to it that to back out now is not an option.

He takes your waist with both hands, fingers squeezing your hipbones, and pushes you away from the fridge and against the wall. You thump and bounce back into him, your body firm, your skin soft.

Now, uncertainty is concern, even fear, and whoever is headed for the kitchen is almost here and words push open your mouth.

You aren't going to scream, no reason to get dramatic and make a scene, but you have to let your presence be known and then you could start explaining this away that Uncle Mike has been drinking too much and doesn't know what he's doing.

He grabs the knob to the walk-in pantry, pulls the door open and pushes you inside, closing the door behind him, your bodies pressed together in the small space, cans of sauce and boxes of pasta stacked behind you, and his hand finds your mouth, fingers smushing your lips against your teeth. Your breath tickles between his fingers. You smell of sweat and perfume so light it might be his imagination.

You squirm against him but freeze at his exhale of pleasure. He wants you to move that way again, a tease of body.

Whoever it is enters the kitchen.

"Shhh," he whispers and leans very close, nose-to-nose. He is beer, onions, and hotdogs, and also something else. An acidic vomit stench you remember perfectly because you'd never forgotten it. Sunlight outlines the door, and a distant star of it reflects in your eye.

"Relax," he says. "It's Uncle Mike. No reason to freak out."

Your breath pushes between his fingers—in and out—rapid. His other hand grips your hip bone and his thumb pushes under the waistband of shorts and underwear.

Pinpoints of red burn in his black eyes.

"I'm going to do something nice for you, okay? I know your dad has been in a bad spot lately. You're like a daughter to me. I'm going to pay for your college. Can't tell your dad, though. He's too prideful."

Breathing the way you are, your chest pushes against his arm over and over.

Footsteps in the kitchen, approaching the pantry.

You make a small, desperate squirrel sound and he pushes completely against you, his arousal urgent, and you two are cheek-to-cheek.

"You're so fucking beautiful," he says. His voice drops several octaves. His hot breath in your ear. "Always have been since you were a little girl. So amazing to watch you grow into a woman."

The footsteps near, stop, and continue—right out of the kitchen and back to the party.

You're breathing so fast it feels like you're suffocating and he tells you to calm down, everything is okay, you're a woman, no reason to be scared, not a little girl anymore, like the one who used to sit on his lap and let him tickle you until you were writhing pleasurably or the one who hid her face in his armpit when you two watched a movie where monsters leaped from the dark.

"You're going to make some man very happy one day. You're like a Nordic goddess, a Scandinavian beauty in whose name Vikings waged war."

It is one of the stupidest things anyone ever said to you, something to be mocked, but the voice is not human. Maybe Uncle Mike is still inside this body but the monster has control. The same monster that possessed Mr. Reynolds, your old gym teacher whose hand slipped too far along your leg.

"Don't you think you're beautiful?"

He wedges two fingers onto your tongue and you gag. He feels your whole body spasm against his.

"Remember when you were thirteen and I found you kissing your teddy bear?" You shift and he pushes you harder against the shelves. A can wedges into your back. You feel cold and breathless and there is no way to stop this. If you fight back, he might really hurt you. "I asked if you wanted to practice kissing a real person and you said 'yes.' You were so embarrassed and I said it was our little secret. That's all this is—our little secret."

You feel sick.

It's Mr. Reynolds all over again, only this is Uncle Mike, someone who has been so much a part of your life. Had he always imagined having this moment with you? What other moments does he imagine?

Is this just how men are?

They see, they want, they take.

If so, what are you supposed to do?

But you know—it's reflex.

The bottle of spiked lemonade smashes into his head and shatters in a dull, liquid crash. He releases you and stumbles back, and you shove him hard to the side, paw at the door handle, can't get a grip as if it is slicked with oil.

He growls, deep and predatory.

Your fingers grip, seize, and you fling open the door.

Light splashes over him and he recoils, turning his head, squinting, but you see the teeth jutting from his gums.

The fangs. Slippery and dripping.

He makes a reach for you, but you are gone, bare feet slapping in rapid gunfire, fleeing into the light where maybe the monster won't get you.

26

AS I READ, THE NIGHT darkened, and now it swaddled the house, thick and warm. Next door was dark, the yard beyond as well, no chanting, circling women. And above us, whatever was or wasn't there had gone quiet.

"Another truthful lie," Jo said.

She was the perfect audience. I would've guessed she'd get bored or her thoughts would fold inward, self-consumed, and she'd interrupt me with a soliloquy, Lady Macbeth's "Out, damned spot," perhaps where she's trying to clean her hands of imaginary blood.

Instead, I felt her eyes on me the entire time, yet I was strangely calm, my voice detached in a way that allowed it to read my words with just the right intonation.

Her lips were moving as I read as if repeating each word to herself after I said it, and maybe that was odd but it felt complimentary. My words had meaning for her.

She got me a glass of water. It smelled a bit sulfuric but I was thirsty enough to drink whatever she put in front of me.

"Did your father ever find out what happened?"

"Enough of it, I think."

I really did have an "Uncle Mike," except he was Uncle Max, and he really did do that to me in the pantry during my graduation party.

I wasn't a gymnast or a cheerleader, obviously, and I don't have tattoos, nor did I smash a bottle over Mike's head and he didn't have black, menacing eyes, but he was still a monster and I was still scared. I didn't tell Dad, but he caught on to something, seeing how I avoided Max whenever he visited, how I stayed well out of hug-reach, and they must've had it out eventually because Uncle Max never came back. I saw him once at a gas station but I looked away before he could say anything.

"Tell me about your father."

"What about him?"

"Is he a good man?"

"Sounds like a trick question."

"Clever girl." She winked at me. "And your mother?"

"She died when I was eight."

"Which makes you daddy's little girl."

It sounded nasty the way she said it, a foul taste in the mouth. I shrugged. Any response feeling like a trap.

"All men bare the burden of civilization's history of violence against women. Massacred by the thousands. Raped by the millions. Genital mutilation. Forced abortions. Forced pregnancy. We are survivors of a legacy of man's brutality."

Her words practically a direct quote from that book: *Today's man is the legacy of yesterday's brutal conquerer.*

"And we women must carry the weight of that victimhood. We all have trauma caused by men. Every woman does. We're pincushions for men. Toys for their dicks."

"That can't be all men."

"Inside *every* man is a toxic male."

"I don't . . . believe that." My father wasn't a toxic male. Colin was a good guy. Right?

"All men are monsters in disguise," Jo said. "Your gym teacher, Mr. Sams. Your Uncle Max. Two men among millions of others. Most men never do anything worse than demean us, speak of us like we're idiots and whores. But it doesn't take much for nasty words to become vile catcalling and for that to become assault and rape. In your stories, you've made them into literal monsters, fangs included."

"I guess. It was just a way to tell a story."

"It was a way for you to process trauma."

I'm not traumatized, I wanted to say. Even as that sentence started to pronounce itself, my skin creeped along my thighs and onto my hipbones.

Steady.

You're so fucking beautiful.

"You understand men are dangerous."

"Women are dangerous, too," I said.

"Oh, yes, indeed." She slurped up the last of her tea, trying to hide her smile around the cup rim. "Read me another," she said.

"Another . . . ?"

"Story, yes."

"Really?"

"Yes, but let's go somewhere more comfortable."

27

THIS TIME I FOLLOWED HER into the room opposite the one with all the heavy paintings. This is where all the candles were, and the chandelier hanging from the coffered ceiling. As much old furniture cluttered up the floor space in here and where we walked the throw rug was worn near tatters. This was also where the pile of clothes was, dresses and shoes, wigs, necklaces, a tiara.

No thick-framed paintings obscured the walls in here; instead, the faded wallpaper was a gray-smeared mural that might've been clouds or a foggy night or so aged it no longer had a subject, but then the silhouette of a woman slipped from that grayness, a candle in her hand, her nightclothes wisping about her, the single flame haloing her path from left to right past the fireplace to the connecting wall where three shadowed figures crouched.

"That's *Macbeth*," I said.

"Lady Macbeth, yes," she said. "And the witches, of course." She gestured to those shadowed figures, hunched together, their garments blacker than the night around them. "You should see it when the candles are lit."

There were candles on stands, on tables, and several elaborate wax-coated candelabras, but there were also candle sconces on the wall I now saw, the mural wrapping around and incorporating them so perfectly I hadn't noticed. There was even one set precisely where Lady Macbeth held her candle.

And even in the spill of poor lamplight, I saw something else.

"That's you. That's *you* as Lady Macbeth."

She glanced at it and then sat in a large red Queen Anne chair. "I was once a beautiful woman, if you can believe it."

The Jo Rose on the wall was slender with a youthful blush in her pale cheeks. The coloring was faded but that redness in her cheeks shone through and the dark glare of her eyes in which a candle flame reflected.

"It's a beautiful work," I said.

"Thank you for not saying I'm still beautiful."

Was she screwing with me, trying to make me uncomfortable? Should I apologize? Was she just a weird old woman being herself?

"Have a seat and read to me."

The only available place was another uncomfortable-looking chair with ornately carved legs and dangling frill around the seat.

"You're sure? It's getting late."

Was it, though, or did it only feel late? Ms. Rose looked a lot more awake than I felt.

Not enough air in here, I thought. *Like the air inside a coffin.*

"You must be tired," I said.

"To be old is to be tired. I could retire to bed but I don't sleep much even if I am in bed. I'm quiescent like a butterfly. I lie there dormant for a few hours, a butterfly resting beneath a leaf."

A cannibalistic vampire butterfly. I touched my palm where she'd cut me.

"You really want to hear another one?"

No one had ever wanted to hear me read one of my stories, never mind three of them. My entire published oeuvre thus far. Even Dad and Emma had read my stories but never asked me to read them to them.

Not that I'd volunteered.

"Don't make me beg. Read me another story. I want to hear it."

28

"Beach Walk"
By Haley Fields
Originally published in WHAT?!, *January 2023*

IF THERE'S A SCREAM IT is lost to the rhythmic slap of the waves.

Whatever the sound, it was at least suggestive of a scream, a seagull's screech perhaps, and you look away from the orangey sun melting into the ocean to the long stretch of beach you've already walked.

Had it really been a scream?

Probably not, and certainly not from the old man who'd been making good pace walking with a cane in the opposite direction.

"Beach walking is for the young," he'd said. "Especially after sunset."

You smiled at him because he reminded you of Grandpa. Not just because he was tall and bald, not just because his baggy sweatshirt was grease-stained, not just because of the cane, either.

There'd been a similar look in the eyes. Even in the sunset light you saw it. Kindness.

Grandpa, who never reduced you to "such a pretty girl" the way everyone else in the family did, who actually asked you about the books you were reading, who actually wanted to read the stories you wrote, who was never awkward hugging you when puberty wreaked hell with your body.

"It's lovely out here," you said to the old man. "Can't beat the view."

He looked out onto the Atlantic Ocean, a stunningly gorgeous evening in late June, the day's ninety-degree-plus heat and blistering sun a memory your sunburned face will remind you of for days.

"I better hurry. The sun's almost gone," he said. "And I can't run the way I used to."

Then he was caneing his way down the beach headed the way you'd come and you were wondering if the worried look on his face was something you imagined.

What had he meant, not running the way he used to? Why would he need to run?

But that isn't the real question, and his worried expression made that clear. The real question is what would he have to run from?

You have your own things you're running from, though admittedly it's a bit dramatic. Back at the rental, Augustus is probably well into the tequila and bad-mouthing you to all your friends as a prudish cock-tease.

Twenty-one and still a virgin, making you both a prized commodity (all boys want a virgin girlfriend) and an irritating liability (all boys want a virgin girlfriend who's horny to give it up).

You're not ready, and why is that such a big deal? *My body, my choice,* you tell yourself.

Besides, it's not like you're a religious freak in chastity underwear waiting for your wedding night. You just don't want to have sex yet. You want to be sure. You want it to be special.

Yeah, yeah, you know—you're making it out too big a deal.

Kiki, who lost her virginity at fifteen and never looked back, has been telling you for years that giving up your purity is not what's special, what's special is finding a boy who can get you off.

That sound again. Definitely a scream.

Someone is running toward you, following your barefoot tracks in the sand.

Could it be Augustus running after you to apologize for being a dick?

No, it's a woman, slender, long hair whirling in the breeze.

Not Kiki, either then, who's kept her head shaved since she was eighteen when she got her first tattoo.

Silly to think it's anyone you know. This is summertime in Cocoa Beach, a popular vacation spot just south of Orlando and Cape Canaveral. There must be thousands of vacationers staying in the condos and beach houses along this strip.

Even so, it's desolate on the beach. You, the old man, and this approaching woman aside. The day's sunbathers and volleyball wannabe*ers* are long gone, napping off the heat or slurping on a different kind of heat, like your friends who're knocking off the bottles crowding the kitchen counter like it's a competition.

Let it go, you tell yourself. *Let them have their fun.*

What you really mean is *Let Augustus have his fun,* which means getting hammered until he pukes. And if you ask him not to drink so much he'll give you that hateful look again and say something dickish, *Have sex with me and I won't drink that much.*

Ugh. Good riddance.

Wait. Are you really making a decision? You're really going to break up with him?

The woman has almost reached you, but for the breath of several seconds you're in your own world. The condos and beach houses recede even farther, the warm water wets your toes, the salty humid breeze plasters your long-sleeve shirt, and you feel your future widening with the promise of possibility. This is the moment everything changes for you—a liberated woman, unafraid now and for the rest of your life.

Then the woman is grabbing your arm and the entire world, including the future that for you is never going to come, though you don't know that yet, shrinks to you and this stranger on a rapidly darkening beach.

Her grip is a vice-pinch around your elbow and you freeze and stiffen like a cat seized by its scruff.

The woman's eyes are huge shadows carving into her forehead. She's incredibly thin, her yoga outfit creasing at the hard edges of her bones.

A flesh skeleton, you think. You'll have to remember that, use it in one of the stories you write.

"Phone!" the woman shouts. "Phone! Help!"

Two thoughts pop into your mind immediately. You hear E.T. telling Eliot he needs to "Phone home," and you're certain this woman is foreign, German maybe or somewhere in the Netherlands.

Whatever the reason, these thoughts make you nervous and you can't form any words.

"Phone!" she yells again.

Does she need a phone? Is she in trouble? Someone chasing her?

"I lost my friend's phone right here," she says, desperate, and lets go of your elbow. "I was running. It fell out my pocket." Bent over, she scans the sand, moving fast, her sneakered feet waffling crazy patterns the rising tide washes clear seconds later.

The woman is making desperate animal-like grunts that are really her saying, "Oh, no, oh, no" over and over.

You take out your phone, put on the flashlight, but its headlight glare mirrors the water into funhouse wobbles. Your face looks so alien you recoil.

No way anyone finds a dropped phone like this. It's either out to sea or buried under slaps of wet sand.

"*Oh, no, oh, no.*"

You're looking best you can, but the water is always moving, the sand always shifting. A cell phone on the beach is no needle in a haystack but maybe it is actually worse, especially at night, and add in this woman with her animal-sounding panic, and all you want to do is run back to the beach house and read a book.

"*Your phone!*" she shouts. "*Gimme!*"

This woman, this near-crazed stranger, makes to grab your phone, to snatch it right out of your hand, the hand of a person trying to help, but you even surprise yourself with how quickly you pull it away from her, your backward steps splashing.

"No," you say, sounding like a child. "You can't."

Which is pretty much exactly what you said to Augustus.

She glares up at you, her face fully shadowed yet you sense her animalistic impulse to act without a thought and you seriously wonder what you'll do if she attacks.

She doesn't. This woman is no threat. She's just another scared person in the world looking for something she lost.

How philosophical.

You start apologizing for whatever reason, but the woman turns, grunting again, and runs on down the beach. Within seconds, she's a silhouette in the condo light and then she's gone.

Time for you to head back yourself. Maybe Augustus won't yet be so drunk he can't have a simple conversation.

The breakup talk. You'll try to help him understand and he'll be dismissive, shrug off your efforts, maybe even call you a prude bitch.

Almost makes you want to say fuck it, it's so exhausting. Fuck it and fine. This is what all you men want? Go ahead. You'll spread your legs and let him—

Your foot hits something. Could be a rock but you don't think so. Holy shit. There it is right at your feet.

The woman's missing cell phone.

You're so surprised you almost don't react, but the next wave splashes over it and you yank it out of the sand before it's gone.

You dry it on your shirt.

The phone lights up. The lock screen is a young couple dressed for prom maybe, he in a tuxedo, hair gelled, and she in a short purple dress and strappy heels.

They look happy and you bet they're not virgins. No way a virgin shows that much leg.

God, you hear Kiki say, *you need to just give it up so you can move on. Move on and get off.*

No, what you need is to get this phone back to that woman.

At least something good can happen today.

Except even as you start running after her and yelling "Hey!" some atavistic cavewoman in your mind tries telling you to stop. It's a vestige of primal times, warning us not to go into that dark cave or climb that ragged cliff, and now it's trying to warn you not to go after that woman.

This is the 21st Century, though, and we all know there's nothing to be afraid of at night.

"Hey!" you yell.

It's tough running on the beach and harder at the shoreline where every step is a splashy mush, but you've already caught up to her—and the gang she's encountered.

She might be asking about the phone and they look like they're laughing at her.

There are five of them, teenagers by the look. Three boys, two girls. They're all in shorts except the middle boy, who's also the tallest and has long hair whipping around his face. The boy next to him is bare chested. His skin is bluish grey in the light spilling over from the condos. The two girls are skinny and showing a lot of skin, both in jean shorts and one in a bikini, the other in a tank top.

The final boy is larger, broad with wide shoulders that stretch the seams of his I ♥ Cocoa Beach shirt. He's laughing the hardest, and you can hear it now, a chuff-chuff cough-like hack as if this kid has lung disease. He's the closest to the woman as well and his stance is one every woman learns early to recognize—he is asserting power, dominance, predatory lust.

"Hey!" you yell again.

You're close enough all heads turn in your direction.

"I found the phone!"

You hold it up, and the woman starts toward you.

I ♥ Cocoa Beach boy clenches her wrist and yanks her back so forcefully she collides into him and he wraps his other arm around her like they're embracing lovers.

Or an animal snatching prey.

He could be showing off the way arrogant boys love to do (Augustus sneaking up behind you and hoisting you on his shoulder and patting your ass), but maybe it's your primal warning system in action.

I better hurry. The sun's almost gone, the old man said. *And I can't run the way I used to.*

You should run. Drop the phone and flee fast as you can to the beach house and your tequila-soaked boyfriend who thinks you're a prude.

But you can't look away.

Mercifully, it's quick, the killing.

Cocoa Beach boy pushes the woman toward the tall one and he seizes her in a spastic hug. His mouth unhinges so impossibly large it must be a shadow, and sharp quills jutting from swollen gums tear out her throat. She's dead before his blood-wet hair whips back across his skull.

Too late now, for her, for you.

They grab you, the girls clawing at your arms, the bare-chested one gashing your shirt wide. You feel the sting of torn flesh and the gush of warm blood.

I ♥ Cocoa Beach sniffs from your armpit to your ear. "Ripe cunt," he says in a wet, phlegmy voice.

He says that because it's what all boys want to say because it's what they're all thinking. They belittle you for the very thing they want.

One of them is pulling off your jeans and underwear and then the girls yank you into the wet sand.

The woman's phone splashes. Your phone is in your pocket, out of reach.

The boy's face is a pale moon filling the sky. He's no boy, and what he pulls from his pants is huge, a thing alien and elephantine.

He tilts his head back for that ugly chuffing laugh to swell his throat in an almost howl. A beast's caterwaul.

He's going to do what he wants to do to you, and then he's going to tear out your throat.

If you're lucky.

Here it is. Finally happening, and it is every bit as awful as you feared. Because this is the horrible truth you always suspected and now know is fact.

It isn't that you wanted your first time to be special; it's your fear that the penetrative violence of the act itself is what made it special. Why boys really wanted it. An opportunity to hurt women.

The girls have your arms pinned in the sand. They're much stronger than they look. Their grins, hungry and lustful, are what scare you more. They want this. They want to see you deflowered, raped, and murdered. They have witnessed this many times before. They have even been the aggressors, perhaps.

This cannot be happening. Please, no.

Such thoughts are childish. As silly and juvenile as hoping you could keep boys away from the one thing they want from you.

It's as primal a need and drive for them as self-preservation is for you.

Can you fight? Is it worth it?

Your hair is wet, the tide coming in higher. You'll drown even if they don't kill you. Maybe that's better, die a virgin, drowned in the ocean like some mythic figure.

Sand buries your hands as the girls push your arms deeper.

Your legs are pushed farther apart.

Here at the end all your fears are as fresh and terrifying as they were when Mommy sat you down and explained why your underwear was bloody and how babies are made.

Please, no. Please.

His face is too long. The eyes sloping and disproportional to his wide nose are black as oil puddles. The mouth is big but not big enough for all those crowding fangs.

You hear a familiar voice calling your name.

Kiki is out here looking for you.

WHAT EVER HAPPENED TO JO ROSE?

If you scream for her and she finds you she will die too.

You aren't going to scream.

You have no weapon. No way to fight.

There is no escape.

I should've let Augustus fuck me, you think. Even if he'd shot his load in you and then abandoned you to get drunk, you wouldn't be out here, wouldn't be about to die. You'd be safe weeping in a bathroom. Crying because you'd finally become a woman.

I'm dying because I'm a virgin.

The monster makes that ugly *chuff-chuff* chuckling sound again, head raised high, mouth open for a porcupine of fangs.

It happens.

He, it, is upon you and *in* you and you can't breathe and the ocean smacks away your tears and you won't scream even if you could because you don't want Kiki to die too, so there's only one thing left to do—tilt your head into the waves for the water to flood your nose and mouth, and all you taste is salt, and this also spreads your pale-washed neck so long that all you are is a frantically pulsating artery lush with blood.

You can hardly wait for the pain of those penetrating fangs when they tear out your throat and the last of your virgin blood splashes into the moonlight.

29

COLIN'S MIDDLE NAME IS AUGUSTUS, so you can take that for what it is. Not that he'd read any of my stories. He asked once not if he could read them but if "You want me to read what you wrote?" and I hid my disappointment in a napkin-wipe across my mouth and said, "They're just silly stories." He never asked again.

The old man on the beach was real, so too the frantic, possibly Scandinavian woman looking for her friend's phone, but the gang of teenagers had done little more than whistle and laugh at me. I hadn't actually found the phone, either, so when the gang passed me I wasn't even saying anything when the tall boy with long hair said, "Hey! You wanna be in a threesome?" "Ew," one of the two girls said. "You wish." The shorter, broad-shouldered guy stared at me and said, "Ripe cunt." Then they were all laughing and the girl who said "Ew" looked at me and when I tried a friendly smile, she flipped me off.

Assholes, not monsters. Still, though, I sensed the possibility of violence among them. It was in the way they carried themselves, youthfully insouciant, swaggering to an unheard beat thrumming in their heads, arrogantly brazen enough to flaunt and heckle like they were kings of this beach.

I'd been afraid of what *could* happen. Had Emma been with me, she would've told them to suck it, and maybe the teens would've laughed. Or maybe they would've attacked.

"That was very sad," Jo said.

"Oh. I was trying for scary."

"It's sad what happened to the brave girl with the good reflexes," she said. "She surrendered. She let those beasts get her on the beach."

"It's not the same girl—"

She waved off my comment. "Of course it is. It's you anyway. So, is that what you believe? Eventually, the monsters get you?"

On my phone, several texts from Colin waited, unread.

"I guess that is pretty depressing."

"Did you consider a different ending?"

I had. In it, the virgin protagonist is not killed but instead initiated into this gang of roving teenage monsters. As the monster fucks her, she fucks him right back, her hips thrusting hard against his, controlling the act, embracing the violent heart within herself, and declaring perhaps a bit too on-the-nose: "*I rape you!*"

The monsters, of course, love that—they welcome her into the cabal and the story ends with my narrator sniffing at the air for victims and hearing the drunken sounds of a boy complaining about his girlfriend who won't give it up. It's Augustus, of course, and he smells ripe for killing.

I liked that ending, but when I tried to write it the scene wouldn't work. It felt contrived. False. Something a man, ironically, might write, believing a woman could harness her sex while being raped and employ it as a weapon.

"This was the ending that worked," I said.

"What if Augustus, drunk and horny, shows up and saves you?" Jo lowered her eyes and her grin raised them back up. "And you watch the monsters rape and kill him instead?"

"That would change things," I said.

"That ending would make me very happy."

"I wasn't raped. It was a scary moment, that's all. Not even, really. They were screwing around, being dicks for their own amusement."

"That's what they think their dicks are for, their own amusement."

On the wall, Lady Macbeth was now right of the fireplace when she'd been left of it before.

Eyes playing tricks, I thought. *She drugged me and I'm hallucinating. That's why I puked. Isn't that what happens when people do ayahuasca? They vomit and shit themselves and then see through the mystical doors of perception?*

"Your stories," Jo said, pulling my focus from the wall, "why use 'you' instead of 'I'?"

"It's a literary thing," I said. "Second person, present tense. The literati love it."

I meant it as a joke, adopting a pretentious persona, but saying it out loud I heard my own desperate need to be accepted, to be regarded as a Real Writer.

"You're distancing yourself," Jo said. "You'll have to do away with that."

Was she giving me writing advice? Not that I was above needing or receiving advice, per se, but those three stories had been published and I felt they were very good.

"For *our* project, dahhling."

"Project?"

"*What Ever Happened to Helga the Hag?* of course."

"You want me to help you write it?"

"Obviously."

"I . . . I've never written a play."

"Words, words, words," she said.

"That's Shakespeare. *Hamlet*," I said.

"To be or not to be." Jo stood. She looked quite awake, like my stories had given her a boost of energy. "Go home and rest. Tomorrow, we'll get started. We have writing to do."

30

OUTSIDE, I STOOD BY MY car a moment. Next door, a light was on in a second-floor room.

A figure moved past the window.

Then came back.

And stared out.

Stay away! She's bad! Bad!

At the cult house, lights were on but all seemed quiet.

The night smelled of—

Ripe cunt.

The light next door went dark behind a cascade of curtain.

The night had thickened and stilled, humidity like congealed gelatin, and I sensed a coming storm, one with violent-blackened thunderclouds that would deafen the mosquito-hum and deluging waters that would pummel and flood the earth and lightning bolts sharp as fangs that could tear open the very throat of the world.

PART THREE:
WHAT EVER HAPPENED
TO HELGA THE HAG?

31

IT WASN'T AS LATE AS I thought, not even midnight, so I texted Colin. He was at Desires, drinking with his buddies but wanted to see me. *Pleasepleaseplease*, he wrote.

I parked in front and texted him. He stumbled out a minute later, laughing, the neon sign painting his face sickly pink. An obnoxious country song blasted out behind him, and I heard his friends cheering him on: "Get some! Get some!"

Colin dropped into the passenger seat. He wore an American flag tee shirt of all things, and he smelled of beer and weed. "Go around back," he said. His words slurred.

"Why?"

He couldn't find an explanation, so he gestured as if I were his chauffeur.

"You're drunk," I said.

He blew a raspberry and laughed.

"Forget it. Go back to your friends."

It took all his limited powers of concentration to turn to me, focus on my face (though his gaze flicked downward several times), and keep his lips from slip-sliding all over his teeth.

"You're really hot," he said.

"Thanks."

My hand caught his chest, kept him back.

"I want you," he said. Drool slipped from the corner of his mouth like he was an actual dog salivating for a treat.

"No," I said, sounding tired and exhausted. "I'll text you tomorrow."

He made a stupid sad puppy dog face and his hand pawed my thigh. "Can I have a kiss?"

I almost relented. I felt bad for him. He just wanted a kiss. Wanted to feel wanted, like anybody else. But if I granted him a kiss it wouldn't stop there. His hands would root out the hem of my shirt and pluck at the button of my jeans.

We're pincushions for men, Jo said. *Toys for their dicks.*

"No," I said, annoyed.

He leaned farther, the alcohol stink strong enough to make my eyes water. His hands went to his own crotch.

"Hey," he said, trying for Mr. Smooth and failing, "don't let this be like Cocoa Beach."

"Oh?" I said, saying it soft, playing along. "What's that mean?"

"You know."

He unbuttoned his jeans and brought my hand toward his crotch.

If he couldn't get in my pants, he would try to make me get in his.

"What do I know?" Still soft, still playing along.

"Don't be scared," he said, grinning. "I want to be with you. I want to be *in* you."

I yanked my hand free and pushed him back, pissed now. I shouldn't have bothered coming here. I should be home asleep.

"Guess not," he said. "You going to run away again? Too bad there's no beach to walk."

"Why're you a dick?"

He made a smirking sound as he closed his fly. "Emma said you've been acting weird."

"Emma? When did you see Emma?"

"Earlier."

"When?"

"She's your friend."

I grabbed his arm. "*When* did you talk to her?"

His lips made a sloppy grin and he went for that kiss again.

Inside every *man is a toxic male.*

I shoved him back.

"Stop!"

"Jesus!" he said, tossing his hands up as if flabbergasted. "What's your problem?"

I took a breath. "When did you talk to Emma?"

He scowled at me, eyes red-rimmed, a tantrum-throwing child.

"What's the point?"

"Of what?"

"You know." His gazed traveled all the way down this time.

"Meaning, what's the point if we don't fuck?"

"Even Emma thinks you're a prude. It's pathetic."

All men are monsters in disguise.

"Get out."

He hesitated, and if he hadn't been drunk he would've tried to repair this conversation, channeled his charm, even apologized, but he saw I was serious and alcohol made him too prideful to play the gentleman.

"You're fucked in the head."

He got out and slammed the door.

I drove home. On the way, I left one hell of a voicemail for Emma.

32

I WOKE LESS THAN AN hour after falling asleep, a startled gasp in my throat.

She knows the truth, I thought.

Not just the story truth, either. She said their names and I hadn't realized. She knew the truth behind the lies of my stories.

Mr. Reynolds was really Mr. Sams.

Uncle Mike was really Uncle Max.

An obvious explanation: Emma told her.

33

DAD MADE ME BACON AND eggs and watched me eat at the table from his usual spot leaning against the counter and sipping coffee. Morning sunshine reflected off the kitchen faucet.

"Another late night?" he asked.

"Not too late." I tapped my phone. No new messages.

"Do me a favor, send me a message if you're out past eleven."

"Is that my curfew?"

"It's so I don't start thinking you're dead somewhere."

"Dad, you pass out by ten."

"But I sleep like shit and when I wake up in the middle of the night I want to see a message from you so I don't have to call the police or load my shotgun."

"How dramatic, John Wayne. I was at Ms. Rose's."

"All night?"

"I'll text you. Happy?"

"Are you?"

A jiggle of egg fell off my fork. "Colin and I had a fight."

"Oh?" He tried to cover his almost-smile with the mug, like Ms. Rose when she was eating ice cream.

"He was drunk."

"Did he . . . *do* something?"

WHAT EVER HAPPENED TO JO ROSE?

If I said yes, Dad would put his coffee down, walk right out of the room to his bedroom closet, fetch the shotgun, and ask for Colin's address.

Or maybe I only wanted to think that's what he'd do. All my talk but in the end I wanted Daddy to protect me.

"No. He was being an idiot is all."

"To quote John Wayne, 'A man deserves a second chance, but keep an eye on him.' Boys today don't know what it means to be a man."

"I bet you'd like to explain it to him."

"You got that right."

Now I was swirling the yolks around on my plate. "I don't know. I thought he was a good guy, but . . ."

"But what?"

"Maybe he's right."

"About?"

"Me."

Dad stood straighter. "What about you?"

"Relax, Dad. It's nothing."

He waited, and I might not have said anything (who would willingly talk about this with their father?), but it just came out.

"He wants to have sex and I don't."

This time, nothing filled the pause.

I heard him approach, felt his unsure hesitation, and then almost cried when he touched my shoulder, squeezed, and released.

"I'm okay, Dad. I don't need anything."

"Maybe," he said trying to find the words, "you know, maybe, if you ever do need help, you can ask your old pops?"

"I don't need saving."

"So much like your mother. Stubborn and courageous."

"Thanks."

Instead of that being that, Dad pulled the chair next to me and sat.

"I don't know if I should tell you this, or if you even want to hear it." He was staring at the mug cupped in his hands. "You know your mother died during surgery, complications from the aneurysm. Before she went into surgery, she could still speak a little."

I touched his wrist. "You told me. She said, 'I love you.'"

He shook his head and looked at me but was seeing something else. "No, she didn't. She said, 'Save me.'"

34

I DROVE PAST EMMA'S. NO cars in the driveway. No lights on. No one home.

Her parents were nice enough, but they'd never been the type to hang around the house. They were always on the move, always something to do. Even when we were younger, her parents always seemed to be off at some event or on some trip or just out with friends. Sometimes they could be gone for days at time.

"They're gone so much you can do whatever you want," I said back when we were teens.

"Yeah," Emma said, "I could kill myself and they wouldn't know for a week or longer."

The night we watched *Cabin Girls* on VHS in her basement, Emma's parents weren't home. They returned the next morning. They brought bagels and donuts and coffee, and I remember how it seemed so cool, her parents bringing all this home for breakfast when my father would've fetched the cornflakes from the pantry, but Emma picked at half a bagel and left me alone in the kitchen with her parents.

For someone who was alone a lot growing up, maybe it wasn't so surprising Emma needed time by herself.

Then again, maybe I should've been a bit more concerned.

35

MS. ROSE HAD NOT LIED about her past. At least not the acting part of it. I easily found several articles about her, including *The Times* review of her off-off Broadway performance in which they called her 'stunningly vivid, appealing, and terrifying,' but the reviewer also remarked that "such a vivaciously virtuosic display of cunning viciousness catapults Lady Macbeth to fiendish heights that threaten to undermine the title character's descent into tyrannical evil which undercuts Shakespeare's great tragedy."

Word salad, my creative writing professor would've said.

"And too much salad gives you the shits," I said.

At the library I had access to all sorts of research and journalistic databases, and I spent most of my day burrowing down various rabbit holes that led nowhere.

Josephine "Jo" Rose was a lifelong Warrenville resident. She was well known in the "professional amateur theater community," whatever that was. And it was her performance as Lady Macbeth that gave the local playhouse a "guaranteed money-maker, year in and year out."

She never married, never had any children. A profile article in an acting magazine quoted her saying, "An actor has no time for romance or parenting. She must give her whole self over to the stage.

Nothing is greater than art."

Her final performance at the Warrenville Playhouse was October 31, 1990. It was a sold-out show and the accompanying picture with the article in the local paper showed her on stage for her curtain call, the entire audience on their feet; you could almost hear the thunderous applause and cries of "Bravo!"

Then she fell out of the modest limelight.

Until . . .

PLANNED *MACBETH* SEQUEL TO STAR LOCAL ACTING LEGEND, declared the headline. "Hollywood producer Sylvester Sylvan announced plans for a 'blood-soaked' *Macbeth* sequel in which 'Lady Macbeth gets revenge' and community theater actress Josephine 'Jo' Rose is set to star as the avenging queen who 'isn't as dead as everyone thinks.'" Sylvan, the article said, "believes this production will restore him to cinematic prestige. Such renown is unclear. Sylvan is best known for his 1969 *Frankenstein* ripoff, *The Stalking Thing*, and the 1976 horror splatter-fest, *Cabin Girls*."

I was so surprised for a moment I couldn't believe it.

Some coincidences aren't coincidences at all.

The same guy who made the movie Emma and I watched as giggling middle schoolers and have quoted ever since was the same who forced himself on Ms. Rose.

Who raped her.

How's the box?

Another surprise waited in the next sentence: "This isn't Ms. Rose's first time working with Sylvan as she starred as 'Unnamed Girl Victim #1' in *Cabin Girls*."

"I like 'em tight," I said in a gargling whisper and felt sick.

Why wouldn't she have told me?

But that answer was obvious: *Cabin Girls* is a shitty little horror movie and her character didn't even have a name.

She must've been one of the girls already tied up in the cabin when the main characters arrive. The hillbilly slaughters those tied-up and gagged girls while singing the Sam Cooke song "Only Sixteen."

I wouldn't have mentioned that role either.

The *Macbeth* sequel did not appear again until the article announcing Sylvan's death—"B-Horror Producer Dead"—which referred to the "blood-soaked *Macbeth* sequel" as the "schlock director's last grasp at B-horror fame" that "ended up on the cutting-room floor, or more correctly, the killing-room floor."

WHAT EVER HAPPENED TO JO ROSE?

That seemed rather cruel for a death announcement, but I guess it's after you're dead when the vultures come to feed.

None of that was what mattered. What grabbed my attention was the cause of death.

"Sylvan, who was known for his questionable behavior and prurient interests, was found dead in an L.A. motel from an apparent drug overdose. He also appeared to be sexually mutilated but authorities do not suspect foul play."

They probably said good riddance.

I wanted more details. How was he sexually mutilated? To what extent? Could it have been The Gelder all those years ago? A first attempt? An attacker getting a taste for it?

And yet the police did not suspect foul play? Did men want to be sexually maimed?

Jo said the producer died from colon cancer. Why would she lie when she knew I could easily discover the truth?

That answer was obvious as well: *She wants me to find out.*

"Because she's The Gelder," I said.

36

"SOMEONE SAY 'GELDER'?"

I should've been more prepared for someone to sneak up on me, it's really the only way anyone approaches anyone in a library, but I was so focused I didn't sense anyone until it was too late.

Call that symbolic, if you want.

I was thinking that for Ms. Rose to be The Gelder, I'd have to accept that she killed Sylvan when she was sixty and, more to the point, had been attacking and castrating men currently *as a woman in her seventies.*

"You're getting obsessed with it, aren't you?"

It was Gabi, the woman with her glasses perched in her thick black hair, Ms. Patriarchal Corruption PhD.

"I heard you say it."

"What?"

"Gelder. Did she strike again?"

"They know it's a woman?"

"I'm being hopeful," Gabi said. "Don't they say you have to grab life by the balls?"

"I guess."

"And I'm returning your book." She held up *Slaying the Masculine*, its cover one of the dumb cartoon caricature caveman ogling a well-

107

endowed woman in business attire. *To get what you want in a man's world, you must think like a man.* "Wouldn't want to get any late fees."

"Right," I said.

"Maybe that's what I should write about," Gabi said. "Title my thesis, *Gelding the Masculine.*"

"Catchy," I said.

"So were you reading about The Gelder?"

"Not exactly."

"What does that mean?"

"You ever hear of Josephine 'Jo' Rose? She was an actress."

"The one who played Lady Macbeth for, like, forever, right?"

"I've been checking on her the last couple days as a favor for my friend."

"Is she, like, going crazy? Ms. Rose, not your friend, I mean."

"I don't know."

"Oh, that *is* intriguing." She leaned over the desk, chin propped on her joined hands, her gossamer sleeves fluttering.

Something about this woman bothered me. It was the fortune-telling-at-the-county-fair look, I thought. Not because such people shouldn't be trusted but because the outfit felt like a disguise. It was an elaborate form of distraction, like Ms. Rose in that butterfly kimono with her face caked white. So distracting she could take my hand and draw blood before I could react.

"Tell me more," Gabi said.

Why was she interested?

Or maybe that was my imagination. The storyteller's mind. Always seeing conflict. Suspecting subterfuge.

That made me think of last night with Colin. He'd been drunk, yes, but was our fight my fault? Had I *wanted* conflict? And if that was true, didn't that mean something was wrong with me?

"Hey," Gabi said. "You still with us?"

"Sorry. What was I saying?"

"That Ms. Rose might be crazy."

I started to speak, stopped. "You know her."

Gabi gave me a coy look and then parted her hands in a you-got-me gesture. "She has a reputation."

"How do you know her?"

"Life-long Warrenville resident." She paused, considering. "And she lives next to that women's shelter, which I hear might be a cult."

Stay away! She's bad! Bad! I saw the two tall figures walking that woman back to the stocky one who touched her face the way you might a cowering animal or frightened child. *She's a monster. She'll make you one too!*

"Oh?"

"You haven't heard anything like that? Didn't see anything?"

"Rumors," I said.

She leaned closer, the way Emma had in this same spot, one woman sharing a secret with another, call it the conspiratorial feminine position. "My friend said the women do weird things there. Ceremonies. Chanting. Dancing. My friend thinks they're witches."

When I was in Jo's kitchen, I'd seen women outside moving in a circle holding hands. *Hand in hand, thus do go about, about.*

"I hope it's true," she said. "I'd call it a win for women."

"Maybe they're doing yoga," I said.

She caught her burst of laughter, stifled it. "You're a smart one," she said. "I like you."

"Thanks," I said.

But I don't trust you. You're keeping tabs on me.

This all seemed too . . .

Coincidental?

"Hey," she said the way you do when you want an idea to sound spontaneous, "are you going there tonight, to Ms. Rose's?"

I nodded.

And if Emma never responded to my texts, maybe I'd be stuck with Ms. Rose for a long, long time.

"They'd be perfect, don't you think?"

"Who? Perfect for what?"

"The women there. For my thesis. Who better to talk to about the oppressive patriarchy than women who have tried to escape it? No matter what they're really doing, it sounds like an attempt to reassert matriarchal dominance, right?"

"Sure," I said.

"Maybe you could scout it out for me? Knock on the door, talk to them, see what happens?"

"I don't think I'd be comfortable doing that." I was thinking of women who were six-feet tall and another whose hand might slap as easily as caress. "It's your thesis, you should do it."

"I can't. Already tried. They turned me away."

"You don't think they'll turn me away?"

"Not if you have a good story."

"Such as?"

"You're the librarian. You must know lots of *stories*."

She emphasized that last word, and that's what convinced me.

It was suddenly so obvious: this woman was connected to the women's shelter or cult or coven or whatever it was. She was here as a spy because of what I'd seen the other night.

Except . . .

She'd been here all week, *before* Emma even asked me about Ms. Rose.

If my suspicions were right (assuming my imagination wasn't leading me off the plank's edge of paranoia), what was I supposed to think?

They targeted me.

But why?

Her spot at the table, the stacks of books, notes scribed on yellow pads, working on her thesis—it was all cover.

She was messing with me. Scout out the supposed cult? See what happens? It was her winking. *I know what you're up to,* she was telling me.

"What do you think I'll find?"

She made a *who knows?* gesture. "Probably just women doing yoga, like you said. Unless they really *are* witches."

"I'll have to bring a broomstick," I said.

Gabi, if that was her real name, returned to her table and to her research, presumably, but I couldn't focus again on what I'd been doing.

I kept looking over at Gabi, trying to catch her looking back.

37

MS. ROSE WAS IN COSTUME again. Not the kimono this time, but a sparkly gold robe with fluffy white cuffs and a matching head scarf wrapped like a turban. She'd gone heavy with the eye shadow and turned her thin lips into crimson worms.

"Hello, dahhling," she said in the doorway. Her eyes were so wide I felt like a mouse trapped in a cat's killer sights. "Alright, Mr. DeMille, I'm ready for my close-up."

When I didn't respond, she dropped the act as easily as shedding the robe she wore.

"Norma Desmond? Gloria Swanson? Really, is a bit of culture too much to ask?"

I knew the reference. *Sunset Boulevard.* I was just too distracted to respond.

She sighed, heavily, dramatically, and then stepped back and grandly gestured. "Come in. We must write!"

38

SOME ASSUMPTIONS PROVE CORRECT.

An antique Royal typewriter waited for me on the kitchen table. It was bulky, looked like it might weigh fifty pounds. Had she carried this thing in here herself? Where had it been?

That was a pointless question. It might've been right in front of me in either of the living rooms and I wouldn't have noticed it among all the other sepia-toned artifacts of decades long past.

Next to the typewriter was a ream of fresh paper and a small pad of ruled pages and sharpened pencils.

Had she gone to the store? Had them delivered? Was someone doing her shopping for her? I never thought to ask.

"I've never used a typewriter," I said.

"We learn as we go," Jo said. She pulled the chair out and waited for me to sit. "Same as art, same as life."

I had no intention of actually writing something for her, but I needed to earn her trust somewhat and she might let her guard down enough to tell me what the hell was really going on. I needed to know why she lied about that producer and what connection if any she had to the women's cult.

She's an old woman. Nothing is going on other than her trying to stave off loneliness and you're turning it into some surreptitious sinister plot worthy of one of those old movies she keeps talking about.

Maybe.

Or maybe I was right. The imagination is a powerful tool.

"Okay," I said. "What do you have so far?"

"I can already feel it," Ms. Rose said. "The room is alive with the electricity of creation."

"*What Ever Happened to Helga the Hag*, is it?"

"My greatest role! My return to the theater!"

Was she in character now or was she talking about herself?

What if there's no difference? I thought.

"I mean, typed. What do you have typed so far?"

She looked incredulous. "I'm no typist."

"Nothing is written?"

"You have the words, and I have the story. It'll be glorious."

"What is the story?"

"It lives in the mind. It's all right up here." She touched her forehead and leaned toward me. I smelled her perfume, something as old and dusty as her home. "Together we shall give it permanence on the page."

"Oh-kay," I said, "what's the story?"

While she explained, I figured out how to roll a sheet of paper into the typewriter and typed out the title page. The keys clacked loudly. The ink was faint but readable. It took a moment to figure out that to get to the next line, you had to use the jutting metal lever on the side to push what's called the carriage into position, which took a lot more effort than hitting the RETURN key on a computer.

```
         What Ever Happened to Helga the Hag?
                        A Play
                By Josephine "Jo" Rose
```

"Add yourself, of course," Jo said over my shoulder. "We're in this together, darling."

```
                         And
                     Haley Fields
```

The story might be pitched as *Arsenic & Old Lace* meets *The Silence of the* "liver and fava beans" *Lambs*. In it, our title character Helga is, much like Jo, a renowned and once-adored Shakespearean actor who longs to be on the stage with her name in the marquee lights. She lives alone in a big old house filled with antiques. A journalism student visits her every day to write up a profile piece on her for class. And then, according to Ms. Rose "they get entangled in a game of psychological intrigue and murder."

"Who do they murder?" I asked.

"Men, of course." Her expression said that should've been obvious. "Helga's cheating husband, for one. The journalism student's boyfriend. The detective who gets suspicious. And they bury all the bodies in the basement."

"Are there bodies in your basement?"

She laughed, high and light and completely fake. "Charming. Use that humor. Audiences love to laugh. Type! Type! *Type!*"

It was slow at first but I found a rhythm and though I hadn't expected to do any actual writing beyond taking dictation, I couldn't help myself. Writing works that way sometimes. The storyline was simplistic and obvious, but it grabbed my interest anyway. When the journalism student, whom I named Annie, after my mother of course, asks Helga "If you could change anything about your life what would it be?" and the old hag replies, "I would've killed a lot more men," I was hooked.

Was it sensationalist? Over the top? Melodramatic? Campy?

Absolutely, and it was the most fun I think I'd ever had writing.

The three stories I'd read to Ms. Rose had each been like bouts of painful constipation, an apt metaphor when you're sitting and trying to squeeze something loose.

This was liberating.

Despite the annoyance and manual effort (or maybe because of it), I started to really enjoy the physicality of typing on this ancient machine. I could hit the keys hard and it produced a wonderfully significant *CLACK!* that gave each letter more gravitas than a computer keyboard or certainly a phone's touch screen ever could. And when Helga declares to Annie that "All men are secretly afraid of what women might do, especially to them," the keys were *CLACK-CLACKCLACK*ing in rapid gunfire that echoed all around.

This is what writing should be, I thought. *Loud. A declarative tumult erupting into the world.*

39

SCENE 2
Primary Sitting Room. Night.

Late. They've been talking for hours, ANNIE furiously taking notes. HELGA wears a different elaborate grand dame costume.

ANNIE: But what is anyone supposed to do about men? I mean, what do we do about the violence they've done to us?

HELGA: There is only one way to stop male violence.

ANNIE: Education?

HELGA: Violence.

ANNIE: You mean . . . ?

HELGA(pause): Murder a few.

ANNIE: Wouldn't that make us as bad as the men?

115

WHAT EVER HAPPENED TO JO ROSE?

HELGA(with theatrical gusto): I dare do all that may become a woman. Who dares do more is none. Will you be a woman with me? Will you dare to finally be violent back?

They stare at each other. After all that has been shared, the traumas, the pain, there is little doubt what the answer will be . . .

ANNIE: And if we fail?

HELGA(a knowing grin): Screw your courage to the sticking place and we'll not fail.

ANNIE: How do we do it?

HELGA moves downstage to the large window over-looking her estate. She faces the audience.

HELGA: Come, you spirits that tend on mortal thoughts, unsex me here, and fill me from the crown to the toe top-full of direst cruelty.

ANNIE stands upstage. She picks up the firewood ax. Its shadow looms huge behind her.

HELGA(shouting): My greatest role! And I do it all for you wonderful people out there in the dark. I do it so you will never forget. I could've been one of the greats!

As her words reverberate all around--
BLACKOUT.

40

HOURS PASSED.

Sometimes writing is like you're squeezing yourself through a narrow chute, your shoulders almost too wide to make it through, you can feel them being compressed, and there doesn't seem to be enough air, and then sometimes when the writing is going well it's as if all at once that narrow tunnel opens into a huge cathedral hall, an enormous room of grand possibility, so vast you might take flight, arms out to glide on a sky of air.

Does that sound ridiculous? Then you've never experienced it.

My fingers were sore and my armpits wet. But I was exhilarated.

Ms. Rose was exhilarated as well, walking up on her toes around the kitchen and clapping her hands the way an excited child might.

"We're really doing it," she said. "It's so wonderful."

I had to use both hands to sip the tea she'd given me. "I think it's really good."

Do you? a voice in my head asked. *Or are you trying to fool yourself? Pretend that writing this stupid play is actually worth your time because you're too scared to do what you said you would.*

"Ms. Rose—"

"Jo."

"Yes, Jo."

She waited.

So did I, waited for my brain to force my vocal cords to push out the words through my mouth.

"Have some more tea, darling."

It smelled of sour feet but tasted okay.

"Elderberry tea," Jo said. "Helps grease these old joints. You were about to ask me something. I could tell. What is it?"

Are you castrating men?

I started to ask about the B-horror producer and cut myself off. "What is it about that women's shelter next door?" I asked.

She'd been pacing the kitchen while I wrote, blurting out dialogue for me to use or not (she never seemed to check), and now she stood with her back to me looking at the broken cuckoo clock.

"They shelter women," Jo said, back still to me.

"You know them?"

"A few."

"Someone named Gabi?"

She was fiddling with the clock, tapping it, tugging on one of the chains.

"This clock," she said, "used to keep excellent time. Timing's important, especially for an actor. You have cues, of course, but there's also the timing an actor keeps in her heart. It must beat in rhythm with the soul of her character."

She lightly punched the clock.

The gesture also punched out my real question: "What really happened to that producer?"

She hit the clock again and the tiny doors parted and the little bird popped out, sang a few chirps, and vanished.

"There," she said, turning to me. "Back in rhythm."

Behind her, the clock's pendulum tick-ticked in its arc. I felt that ticking inside my chest, screwing with my heartbeat.

"You were asking about that awful man?"

"Yes, how did he—"

"The one who *raped* me?"

She went to the counter behind me and turned back and stopped.

"You said he died of colon cancer."

If there'd been any light coming in through the window, her shadow would cast large on the wall. What might I see? A carving knife held high? An icepick?

Why not an ax? Hell, if I was going to go that far, why not assume

118

this old woman was a serial killer who buried her victims in the basement?

"He died in an L.A. motel from a drug overdose," I said.

"And . . . ?"

"And?" I said.

"You must've found out the rest."

"He was sexually mutilated," I said.

"Isn't that wonderful?"

My heart was doing a weird skip-beat, my brain felt like it was being squeezed, but my breathing was so far (*steady*) calm.

Ms. Rose wasn't going to hurt me, certainly wasn't going to try to kill me. I was her writing partner. She needed me.

Good old rationalization again.

I turned enough to look up at her. No knife. No ax. Just an old woman holding a cup of bad-smelling tea.

"Did you do it?" I asked.

She sipped from the cup. "How would Helga answer that question?"

That unblinking stare. My palms felt slick.

Our eyes locked and the moment felt as if it might never end. I'd called her out, challenged her to confess or do even something homicidal, and I did it while seated at the kitchen table with her directly behind me.

In perfect killing position.

She might be old, and she might not be The Gelder, but she could smash that tea cup down into my face and use a broken shard of it to stab my throat again and again, blood spurting onto us and speckling the typed manuscript on the table.

"Helga would say, 'When a man gets what he deserves, we don't ask why or how or who. We rejoice,'" I said.

"That's perfect," Jo said. "Write that down."

For a moment I did nothing, couldn't tell if she was challenging me right back, daring me directly to accuse her, but even through the fear I knew she was right and my creative impulse insisted I do as she said.

It *was* perfect. I knew exactly how that line could be used—first when Annie confronts Helga about what really happened to her previous husband (a seedy, sleazy producer) and then after they both murder her current (also seedy, also sleazy) husband and then finally at the end, Annie, slathered with her boyfriend's blood, will say those

119

words to the detective who arrives a moment too late to stop the violence.

I scribbled all that down on one of the pads. I pressed so hard one of the pencil points broke.

"That's a good girl," she said.

Ms. Rose patted my shoulder, gripped it.

The clock *tick-tick*ed.

That's when we heard the footsteps on the stairs.

41

YOU KNOW SOMETHING BAD IS coming. You know that we never finished the play, Ms. Rose never graced the stage again, you know The Gelder was caught, but what you don't know is how it happened.

Someone else really was in the house, and as those creaking steps descended, I knew I never should've come here at all.

My imaginary audience *should* be heckling me—*You deserve what's coming!*—but whoever thinks they really are in a horror movie until they see the monster for themselves?

42

"WHO ELSE IS IN THE house?" I asked, my voice trembling.

Ms. Rose squeezed my shoulder.

Steady, a man's voice said in my head.

You're so fucking beautiful, said another.

Ripe cunt, said the last.

The footsteps echoed so much more loudly than could be possible.

They were coming down the hall now—measured, deliberate.

Steady.

"You're so scared. It's what the men have done to you," Jo said. She spoke slowly, clearly, no theatrics required. Her voice was soft enough to hear the steps getting closer. Closer. "Touched you. Cornered you. Reduced you to a plaything. Damaged you. Terrorized your own womanhood. But now it's finally time to be brave."

Out of the shadowed hallway, a figure stepped into the light.

She wore pink nurse's scrubs. Her hair was pulled back in a taut ponytail.

"How's the box?" Emma said from the archway.

"Tight," I said in barely a whisper.

"I like 'em tight." No hillbilly voice this time.

Ms. Rose's hand on my shoulder. A bead of sweat rolling down my ribs. The kitchen closing in around me. My mouth tasting the way that nasty tea smelled.

"Thought you were studying," I said.

"I've been doing more hands-on work," she said.

She held a wooden box, lifting it now as though it were evidence. It was the same small box Ms. Rose had carried upstairs two nights ago. I saw now that engraved on it was a familiar triple-moon design. Familiar because Emma had a tattoo of it just below her collarbone.

"What's in the box?"

"C'mon," Emma said, "we gotta get next door. They won't wait forever."

"Next door? Why? Wait for what?"

"It's a surprise. Let's go."

Ms. Rose squeezed my shoulder again. "Time to be brave," she said.

43

Same location. Later that same night.

HELGA now wears an elaborate butterfly kimono costume. Her face is painted white. Long eyelashes.
Fake nails. She holds an ax.

ANNIE is on the floor, the last of her confes-
sional weeping spilling free.

ANNIE: He did it. My boyfriend forced himself on
me! He took my virginity!

HELGA: He raped you.

ANNIE: Not raped, but close—

HELGA: Yes. He raped you! Say it!

HELGA goes to ANNIE, stands over her.

HELGA: Don't dare think anything other. That's all
men are good for. Sticking themselves where

124

they're not wanted. Little boys with adult desires. Pure ego. They want so they take. Brutal
conquerors. Rapists. Every last one of them!

ANNIE has stopped crying. She appears changed.
Convinced. She watches HELGA, as if enraptured by
a great performance.

HELGA: To get what you want in a man's world, you
must think like a man. You know what that means
we must do. You've always known it in your truest
heart. Your woman's heart. (Dramatic pause) We
must kill them, dahhhling. We must kill them all!

ANNIE (slowly, building): Yes. Yes! YES!

ANNIE stands and joins hands with HELGA. She
raises the ax in her other hand.

BLACKOUT.

PART FOUR:
THE GELDER

44

ONCE OUTSIDE IN THE DARK yard, I started in on Emma. It was a barrage of angry questions and hurtful insults tangled into a rant where I called her out as a terrible friend, declaring her a sociopath, accusing her of helping Ms. Rose castrate men.

She didn't try to stop me. She let me get it all out and then I was lightheaded and breathless and she was rubbing my back and reminding me to force all the air out through my teeth and then suck it all back in.

"You're okay," Emma said. "I'm here with you. I would never do anything to harm you."

Oh, really? I wanted to say. *We've been friends almost a decade and it's always what can Haley do for you, never what the hell is Emma going to do for Haley!*

But her look was so compassionate it broke my rage and I couldn't do anything except hug her. It felt wonderful, safe.

"How's the box?" she asked.

"Tight," I said, wiping at tears.

She didn't do the hillbilly response. Instead, she said "Okay, good," and then held out the wooden box. "I need your help, but you're really going to be helping yourself."

"Be straight with me."

"I am. Friends are for helping each other, right?"

She gestured for me to take the box. Faint light spilling out from the kitchen gave it a wet sheen. That made the engraving appear to glow. A triple moon. A symbol of feminine power. Or something.

I took the box.

Something inside it, not very heavy. I resisted the urge to shake it and see what sound it made.

"You remember when I dropped out of Binghamton?"

"Of course."

"I almost killed myself. Wanted to."

"What? You never—"

"You would've gotten me help."

"Uh, yeah."

"I didn't want help. At least I didn't think I did. But when I was volunteering at the community center and I met Jo, I found a reason to live."

It broke my heart I hadn't at least suspected Emma had been hurting so badly. What kind of friend did that make me? I was so preoccupied with myself and thinking Emma had her shit so well together that it never occurred to me something could be seriously wrong with her.

The night was so quiet around us, we might've been the only two people for miles.

"I never told you exactly why I dropped out of college. You probably thought I was partying too much, drinking, drugs—boys, whatever."

"No, no, I—"

Luckily, she didn't let me flounder for an answer she'd already guessed.

"I was raped," she said. "Gang raped."

"Jesus Christ. You should've . . . I would've . . . Fuck!"

I hugged her, squeezed hard as I could and almost dropped that wooden box. "I'm sorry I wasn't there for you," I said.

She let me hug her but didn't reciprocate, and once I let go she continued.

"It's so pathetic I feel stupid even saying it, but it's what happened. It was a frat party. He was older. Pretending to be a grad student. He said his name was Kyle but I found out later it was Dominic. Anyway, nothing very surprising—he put something in my drink and I was vaguely aware of him fucking me in some room that stank of sweat

130

and beer. Or maybe that was his smell.

"Other guys were in there watching. Cheering. When he was done he shoved his dick back in his pants and said, 'Next!' I remember that so clearly, him calling out like they were all waiting customers. I guess they were.

"One of them got rough, choking me, and I tried to fight back, and Dominic grabbed my head, pulling my hair so I thought my scalp would tear and he said, 'Stop or I'll make you stop.'

"I don't know how many there were, or how long it lasted, but when they were done they just left me there. Didn't even put a blanket on me. A week later I dropped out of school and came back home."

All my fears, my desperate clinging to my virginity, my horror stories of men as sexual monsters—it was all rooted in the terror of experiencing *exactly* what Emma had gone through.

I'd been molested and propositioned by my father's friend, but Emma had been gang raped.

What kind of world is it when the atrocities men commit against women are so common two best friends are both victims of it?

I thought Emma was a strong, confident, sexually bold young woman, and maybe she was, but she was also a victim of man's brutality, used, abused, and discarded.

She was traumatized, but I saw it in the lively, crazed flicker of Emma's eyes then: She was also insane.

"It's all okay," Emma said. She grinned, actually grinned. "The Gelder took his balls."

Like The Gelder was a hero, a feminine crusader.

Maybe that's exactly what The Gelder is.

I remembered my research.

"Dominic Evans," I said. "That's his name. You're the anonymous source that called him out as a rapist."

Then I just came right out with it.

"You did it. You're The Gelder."

"I wish," she said. "The Gelder is like a myth conjured into reality. An avenging spirit summoned from the very soul of woman."

"Fuck's that mean?"

"Open the box. Take a look."

I didn't want to. I wanted to drop it and run, but it was far too late for that kind of cowardice now.

"What's in here?"

"Go ahead," she said, "look."

"They're in here? His . . . ?"

The box felt suddenly heavy and I almost hurled it away like a live grenade.

"Open it," Emma said.

I did.

What I saw in the box was so unexpected and seemingly incongruous I gaped at it as if I'd never seen such a thing before. The implication should've been obvious but it really wasn't. Not right then.

Inside was a pair of red-handled garden shears. The curved stainless-steel blades gleamed clean and very sharp. It was the kind you held in one hand and it had a coiled spring making those curved blades powerful enough to snip through thick branches. The brand was SnipItAll.

I picked them up. "What is this for?"

But that was obvious.

Oh, shit.

I dropped them back in the box, thunked the lid shut. Sweat squeezed out all over my body like I was in a sauna.

"No, no, no," I was saying and with each exhale I lost breath.

"Oops. Guess you're an accomplice now. Fingerprints."

I tried to speak and couldn't. I fell to one knee.

"Joking," she said. "Sort of."

Emma kneeled before me, put her hands on my shoulders. "It's going to be okay. Seriously. You just have to breathe."

My vision closed in like those old timey movies that circle to black, but Emma shook me. "*Breathe!*"

I did, hissing through my teeth out and in, out and in.

The circling black faded away.

"I know this is a lot to take in," Emma said. "But it's going to be so good for you. I used to have panic attacks, too. You never saw me have them because I saved them for when I was alone. When I was at my lowest and wanted to die. Hey, look at me."

Her eyes were huge coins, reflecting that kitchen light. She wiped at the corner of her mouth. She was drooling. "I don't have them anymore. I don't suffer. I don't hurt. I'm free. You'll be free, too."

"Free?"

She put her forehead to mine. "I found him for you. Retired to some dump near Albany. Redundant, I know. Easy enough to find, though. Especially when he frequents certain websites."

"Found who?"

But there was only one person she could mean. Emma might not have shared her traumas with me, but she'd read my stories, and she knew my truth—the fear I had of those teens on the beach that was really a fear of intimacy with Colin, Uncle Max cornering me in the pantry and how I wished so badly I'd really smashed a bottle on his head, and the man who put his hands on a child where they shouldn't be and whispered a single word that continually thrummed in my pulse.

Steady.

"Come on," Emma said and pulled me to my feet. "Time to be free."

Then she was tugging me across the yard, laughing like we were giggling teens again running off to the practice field to lean on the chain-link fence and whisper about the boys during their football practice.

45

WE WENT IN THROUGH THE back. The layout was almost identical to Ms. Rose's—door into the kitchen, hallway dividing between living and dining rooms to the stairs.

Unlike her home, this one had almost no furniture. An old piano carpeted with dust was the only thing in one room and in another an enormous grandfather clock draped in cobwebs occupied half a wall, but there were no chairs anywhere and the only lights were dangling bare bulbs in the middle of each room.

As in Ms. Rose's, heavy drapes covered the windows.

"This place is abandoned?" I asked.

"Shelter owns it. Looking to expand."

Then we were heading up the stairs, her hand still pulling me along.

The stairs creaked very loudly.

At the top, we turned right and there before us was a closed door with bright white light creasing its outline.

 She grabbed the doorknob.

"Wait," I said. "This isn't real, right?"

"How's the box?" Saying it the hillbilly way.

"I'm serious, Emma."

"I like 'em tight."

Believe it or not, right then was the first time I'd ever realized that the contraction of them as 'em was also an abbreviation of Emma.

"Time to be brave," she said.

And pushed open the door.

46

SOME COINCIDENCES AREN'T COINCIDENCES AT all.

I wasn't thinking at that moment of my creative writing professor's words (I wasn't thinking anything except *OhShitShitShit*), but as I write this now it strikes me as particularly apt. There are coincidences throughout our lives that may not be as coincidental as we think. What goes around comes around, and it shouldn't have surprised me at all that that's exactly what was happening here.

Right out of a low budget '70s horror flick.

In *Cabin Girls*, before the Final Girl makes her stand and defeats the sadistic rapist hillbilly, there's a scene where she shares a traumatic story with the other captive girls about a camp counselor who did terrible things to her and as he did them and she cried and protested he would put his finger to his lips and shush her. *Shhh*. It's the most uncomfortable scene in a movie filled with rape, throat-cutting, and disemboweling because it's the most honest. And the one that scared me the most.

Not only because of what happened to me in that school gym.

But because I was afraid I was just like that Final Girl.

If somehow I ever get the chance to confront that man, she says, *I'm going to take his balls and as he's screaming I'm going to put my finger to my lips and go, "Shhh."*

Can you guess how she kills the hillbilly?
She swings an ax into his crotch.
Again and again.
And again.

47

THIS IS THE ROOM.

A set of caged work lights on a stand loom over the boxspring on which a naked old man is tied spread eagle by yellow ropes to each of the massive bedposts. He is blindfolded, gagged, and Emma's pink Beats headphones cover his ears.

The harsh work lights blanch his skin into something sickly pale and alien, like a creature pulled from the ocean's darkest depths.

The only other thing in the room: a folding TV tray beside the bed, on it Emma's iPhone and a metal tray, and on that tray sharp instruments and syringes and gauze and bandages and blue medical gloves and thick elastic bands and a small culinary butane torch.

"Say hello to Mr. Sams, the *pedo* himself," Emma says, shouting that word pedo but the old man strapped to the bed cannot respond even if he could hear her. "Told you I found him."

You could try to protest, to argue this could not be the same man whose voice had haunted you for years but there is no point. It is him. Even looking as he does, he was the man who'd touched you the way no person should ever touch a child.

You know because of the hands. They're tied so tight by that propylene rope they're bulging brownish red, but there's no doubt. The little girl living inside you recognizes those hands.

The way they touched. The way they violated.

It's Mr. Sams.

Sweat-slicked gray hair sticks to his scalp and more gray hair speckles his flabby chest and sprouts in tangles around his tiny nipples and molds over his ugly potbelly and engulfs his crotch. His penis is a small fat slug cowering in all that hair.

No one else is in the room.

"It's just us," Emma says. "This one is yours. The next one will be for all of us."

You can't speak even if you had something to say.

What does she expect you to do?

"He can't see us. He can't hear us. He's listening to an endless loop of screaming banshee music, as you call it. He'll never know it was you. But he'll know. In his nasty little rotting soul, he'll know."

You smell him now—an old man stink. It reminds you of yellowing-and-moldy old books mixed with dried sweat on a used towel.

"The only way to not hurt anymore is to hurt someone instead."

No, I won't accept that.

But those words don't even come out of your mouth.

Because you know she's right. You should do this. You really should.

"It'll be quick," Emma said. "Real quick. Those blades are sharp."

Blades. The box. Right there in your hands.

Emma catches the box and squeezes it back in your hands. "No backing out now. This is what you need. You have to trust me on this. Open the box. Go on. Open it. It's okay, Haley. I'm right here with you."

When you're frozen in panic, it's ironically easy to respond to simple commands. She peels your right hand free but lets you do the rest.

You open the box.

"Pick them up," Emma says.

The red handles are spongy hard rubber. They fit into your grip perfectly, and when you unlatch the lock you feel the power of the coiled-spring. Both blades are curved, the top one thicker with a hooked point.

Emma takes the box and guides you to the side of the bed.

The blindfold is one of those blackout sleep masks and the bottom is soaked dark with tears. Snot crusts his nose. His lips murmur a ceaseless apology around the tee-shirt gag and it sounds exactly like the way he spoke all those years ago, a breathless urgency, an excitement but one that is now pure despairing terror, and all you can think is that one word which you can't ever forget.

A word Emma now says: "Steady. All you have to do is slide the blades into place and snip-snip. One hard squeeze'll do it. I'll handle the rest."

She sets the box down and puts her hands on your hips to shuffle-step you directly over his crotch.

From this angle, you see she has shaved the hair to expose his balls. They are veiny and sag onto the boxspring between his hairless quivering thighs. There's an old stain on the boxspring that might be spilled wine but isn't. His ballsack is a painful purplish-blue. Several thick rubber bands are wrapped as tight as possible where the scrotum meets the body. You think of how you use bands on plastic bags that no longer seal, how the plastic wrinkles in tight folds and the top blooms like a transparent flower.

This thought makes you ill.

Emma is directly behind you, her body against yours. She slowly pushes your hand. The shears are so bright in this light you squint.

"No," you manage to say. "I can't."

"Come on, Haley. Be brave. What's the point of writing all those stories if it's not to make you be brave when it really matters?"

What does she know about writing? She's never written anything longer than a text message. You were always letting her plagiarize your essays in school. She was always using you. And now she's using you again. Making you not only an accomplice in her madness but a participant.

"*No,*" you say.

Her other hand rests on your back and slowly rubs between your shoulder blades.

"We won't get caught. I promise. It'll all be taken care of. Once we're done, he'll be taken away, dropped in some parking lot miles from here. Another victim of The Gelder."

You've never stared at any naked man, and certainly not an old man, laid out before you like this. He's sickly looking. Sad. Pathetic. He's completely vulnerable. You could do anything to him. Touch him anywhere.

The way he did to me, you think.

"I know you don't think I get it," Emma said, "all your writing, but I do. You write to make sense of the awful shit you've gone through, but writing is another form of avoidance. You're a victim." She paused. She's been practicing this speech. "But you don't have to be. It's time to take control of your own story. It's time to face what happened, what *this man* did to you, and time to take action. Your stories are cries for help. Cries for vengeance." Her hand on your wrist and you don't resist as she guides your hand closer, closer. "Choose vengeance."

The blades slide into position beneath those bunched elastic bands.

Mr. Sams goes rigid. His lips stop. Even though the bands have certainly cut off nearly all blood flow to his testicles, he feels the blades there at his most sensitive and precious of places.

"Puhheeezzee NOOOO!" he begs through the gag.

Fresh tears wet the edge of the sleep mask. Tremors shake his body.

"Once you're free," Emma whispers in my ear, "you can start your life."

He did things to you when you were a little girl that really fucked you up. You've cried so many times for that little girl. You feel so bad for her. You want so badly to protect her but you can't. Things were done to her. Awful things. By *THIS* man. He deserves to be punished and punished severely.

But does that mean cutting off his balls?

What if he's mentally ill? He needs clinical and psychiatric help.

Your hand shakes.

Steady, you think.

Steady.

No. You can't do this. It's wrong and awful and cruel and maybe even evil and he might deserve punishment but not this and you certainly shouldn't be the one doing—

Emma slides a hand over yours. She's wearing a blue nitrile glove.

"He deserves this," she whispers in your ear.

Maybe he does, you think.

The blades do the rest.

48

THE FLESH SEVERS EASY AS wet paper tearing. There is wiry sinew, tough like chewy gristle inside that flesh, but it's no match for sharpened steel.

Mr. Sams screams and screams, tendons bulging in his neck and veins worming through his cheeks and along his temple.

"*Shhh,*" Emma says.

Then he passes out.

There's not nearly as much blood as you would've guessed, but what there is pools on the boxspring, refreshing that faded stain.

You can't get enough air in your lungs. Your head feels so light.

You're going to pass out.

You force air through your clenched teeth just like Dad taught you.

Emma picks up the scrotum and dangles it in your face. A hypnotist with a watch. A child with a hand puppet. A psychotic woman with a man's severed manhood.

You try to breathe in, can't.

"Now, to cauterize the wound," she says and picks up the butane torch.

You're falling but you never hit the floor.

49

I WOKE IN EMMA'S CAR, slouched in the passenger seat, seatbelt cutting across my throat.

We were parked in my driveway. My Jetta was already there.

Emma took a breath, hands on the steering wheel, and turned her head to look at me. "I'm proud of you. It took a little extra nudging at the end, but you did it. That's a good girl."

I was both cold and overheated. My skin prickled with gooseflesh but was also clammy with sweat. My thoughts felt fogged in. I tried to speak. "You . . . You removed his . . ."

"*We*," Emma said. "*We* cut off that pedo's balls."

Air lodged in my throat. The rubbery handles of the garden shears pressed against my palm and I flung my hand out wildly but it was a phantom sensation and my empty hand smacked the dashboard hard enough to hurt.

I couldn't breathe.

My vision darkened.

Good. I'll pass out. Maybe forever.

"Stay with me, Haley. We're in this together."

"No, no, no," my words a faint whisper.

"Yes. You and me. But don't worry. There's others. Lots of others. I'm not, like, some lone psycho. This is a well-oiled machine. And

143

now you're part of it."

"No, no, no, no."

"Yes, yes, yes. This is good for you. Trust me. You're going to wake up a whole new woman. No more scaredy little girl. No more molested and abused victim. No more weak virginal child. You're a woman now."

I fumbled my phone out of my pocket. "Police," I said. "I'm calling. This is insane. Crazy. You're crazy. I won't be a part of it. *Won't! Can't!*"

The slap was so sudden and precise it didn't register until her hand was back on the steering wheel.

A second or two passed before I even felt the sting on my cheek, but my breathing had eased. My panic temporarily halted.

Shadows carved lines through Emma's face like it was made of rock.

"Don't tell anyone. Don't think of calling the police. This isn't just me. There's a lot of us. Besides, your fingerprints are all over the box and the shears. And you were the only one with motive."

Nonsensical protests spurted and sputtered between my lips.

She put a finger to her own. "Like a librarian," she said. "*Shhh.*"

50

EMMA LET ME TAKE MY phone and walk inside by myself. She said she'd call me later. She didn't repeat her warning, didn't slap me again, didn't threaten to hurt or kill me.

Because she knows I'm fucked. And I know I'm fucked.

I went to my father's bedroom but he was asleep. I didn't wake him. If I told him what happened he'd probably not believe it at first and then he'd definitely call the police.

He'd want to call John Wayne, if he could.

I was freezing, so I put on another shirt and then a hoodie. I saw blood—*snip, snip*—on my jeans and the rush of acidic bile up my throat was so immediate I couldn't do anything but lean over and gag on the yellowy mucus dribbling out my mouth.

I put on different jeans.

No way I was going to sleep. I needed a plan. I'm not sure what, if anything, could fix all this, maybe only confession, but I was a writer. I had a strong imagination. I could come up with something.

I just had to think. I paced my bedroom. Thinking. Considering. Time passed but no epiphany arrived. That was okay. I needed to relax and give myself a little more time—

My phone vibrated. A text from Colin. *Can we talk?*

Too tired, I texted back.

145

A moment later, he was calling.

I don't think he'd ever called my phone before.

"Colin, I can't talk about us right—"

"How's the box?" Emma asked. "Is it tight?"

"Emma? What the fuck—?"

"It's later," she said. "Your boy was eager. He was waiting for me. Told you I was right about him. A white van will be outside your house in two minutes to pick you up. Be outside when it gets there or the driver will call the police."

"What? Van? No. Call the police? Go ahead. Do it. I'll tell them everything."

"Really? Fingerprints. Motive," saying the last two words in a sing-songy, mocking way.

"Why are you on Colin's phone?"

"Inside every man is a toxic male. I'm going to prove it to you."

This one is yours, Emma had said. *The next one is for all of us.*

My mouth was swollen and tasted of metal.

Colin was next. He was strapped to that boxspring.

"And if you call the police, it'll be a real shame because you need to be here for this. We're making something special, and I want you to be a part of it."

She waited but I could only produce dry clicking noises.

"Be outside."

No. I wouldn't go. Let them call the police if that's what the plan was. I'd be jailed, sure, and the evidence was against me, also sure, but eventually the truth would come out. They'd interrogate Emma and she'd snap. She'd confess. Hell, she might be proud to.

"Oh," Emma said like she just remembered something, "before the driver calls the police, she's going to call me, and I'm going to cut off Colin's cock and then slice his throat. Don't worry, I'll wear gloves so your fingerprints don't get smudged."

51

A WHITE VAN IDLED AT the curb.

Dangling from beneath the license plate was a pair of those plastic truck nuts. They were neon pink.

I rushed down the lawn, waving my arms, and then pounding on the passenger window.

The driver glanced over. She was on the phone.

"Stop," I said as I opened the door. "Don't call anyone. I'm here."

"She's here," the woman said into the phone and ended the call. "Hop in, Miss Librarian."

For once, the woman was wearing her glasses. Her black hair was an unruly mess and her silky layers were wrapped up beneath a leather jacket.

"Gabi?" I said.

"It's like a professor told me once," Gabi said, "get a PhD. It sure beats working."

52

THERE WAS AN ADVANTAGE TO things moving so quickly:
I had no time to panic.

"You really *were* spying on me," I said.

"Just grabbing life by the balls," she said. "Right, girls?"

In the back of the van were the two tall women I'd seen the other
night escorting the (*She's bad! Bad!*) woman back to the candy-colored
Victorian.

Where the witch lives, I thought. Except that wasn't true. They were
all witches. Ms. Rose. Emma. These women. And now me.

The women were sitting on narrow benches opposite each other
and between them on the floor was a body wrapped in a sheet.

"Is that—?"

"The Gelder strikes again," Gabi said.

Then we were moving.

"He'll be dropped off in a parking lot somewhere," Gabi said,
sounding like it was an afterthought, this man who was sexually mutilated just being dumped in some random lot.

Sexually mutilated by you, a voice reminded me. *You were holding the
garden shears. Maybe it was Emma's hand over yours that applied the pressure,
but it's your fingerprints on the handles. Let's be honest, anyway—it isn't as if
you protested that much. You wanted to do it. You wanted to sever this old man's*

148

balls. You enjoyed it. You reveled in his pain because he deserved—

"Are you even writing a thesis?" I asked to stop the monologue in my head.

"Damn right. Power to the matriarchy. The problem with academics is they never get their hands dirty. No real-world experience." She drummed her fingers on the wheel to some imaginary beat only she could hear. "Like you. You're a librarian. You *read* about the world, but have you experienced it?"

Steady.

You're so fucking beautiful.

Ripe cunt.

"Enough," I said and Gabi wasn't sure exactly what I meant.

53

THE VAN PARKED AT THE curb outside the house between the women's shelter and Ms. Rose's.

It looked completely dark and empty.

But I knew better.

"Let's go," Gabi said. "The night is young."

She left the van idling and got out. For a moment, I had the thought to jump into the driver's seat and speed off, to the police maybe, but one of the tall women was already moving behind the wheel. The other one came up beside me. "Out," she said.

The van drove off before the door even shut behind me.

At the bright Victorian, someone was standing on the front porch but the light was off so they were a shadow in the dark.

"Emma said you did great. You're a natural snipper." She laughed high and light.

Run. I could run.

Straight into prison.

"It's best to do another one right away," Gabi said. "Before you start thinking too much about it."

She grabbed my hand same as Emma had done and pulled me across the lawn to the back of the house, inside, up the stairs, and then I was at that same door again, bright light carving out its shape.

"Go on," she said.

I reached for the knob. Hesitated. What was waiting beyond this door? But I knew, and that's what made it so awful.

Standing beside me, Gabi asked, "What would a man do?"

"Grab life by the balls," I said and opened the door.

54

WHEN WE WATCHED *CABIN GIRLS,* Emma and I giggled our stupid selves silly, wrapped up together in a comforter, chip and pretzel crumbs poking at our arms, and one-upping each other with soda belches, but what I remember so clearly is that before every gory death scene I covered my eyes so I could peer protectively between my splayed fingers and each time Emma said, *Drop your hands and watch it all. See everything.*

I opened the door and saw everything.

Awful as it sounds, the first thing I saw was Colin's erection. I'd seen it before, of course, held it and yes, tasted it, but I'd never seen it like this. He was, like Mr. Sams had been, strapped to the bed by the yellow ropes, and he was blindfolded and gagged and wearing Emma's headphones, but his penis was at full attention, so engorged it was purplish red.

Emma stepped from the wall beside me. "I got him all worked up for you. *Joking.* Sort of. It's a cock ring. Traps all that blood. It's extra tight. Just think, we could snip it right off and it'd geyser blood like Old Faithful."

The cock ring, I now saw, was bright purple and nestled in his manscaped pubic hair.

The garden shears waited on the metal tray beside the bed. Angry rashes spotted and streaked Colin's naked body. Like he'd been hit or whipped. The work lights burned so hot and bright this monstrous spectacle bleached into my retinas.

His clothes were piled by the wall, letterman's jacket on top.

"Believe it or not, Haley, but he was more than willing. Came right over here. Got handsy really fast. Said he always wanted to fuck me. Got naked. I said I wanted to get kinky and he grinned like the stupid little boy he is."

He was not grinning now. He was huffing breath hard enough to blow his lips back from his teeth.

"Fuck him," Emma said.

"He isn't Mr. Sams," I said. My voice could barely squeeze out my throat. "Colin doesn't deserve this."

"No," Emma said. "I mean, *fuck* him. Do it. He's ready to go."

"If you won't," Gabi said on the other side of me, "I will." She elbowed me like this was the funniest thing in the world.

"Take off your jeans and get on his dick. You'll have to spit on it to lube it up but it's plenty hard. Like I said, that trapped blood ain't going anywhere. Unless we want it to."

She made a quick-swipe cutting gesture with her blue-gloved hands.

Blood spotted her pink nursing scrubs.

I couldn't move. This could *not* be happening.

"Emma, no."

"Why not? Virginity isn't something you should give away, not a thing a man gets to take. It's yours to wield. Yours to fuck him with. Get on that dick and conquer him with all the power of the female gods."

"Emma—"

"You know what men are into?" Gabi asked, sounding analytical. "They'll watch any porn, but you know what they really love? Bond age, degradation, humiliation, choking and gagging and rape fantasies and forced anal sex and gang bangs and cum strewn over all of it. Now, let me ask, you think all the women in those videos participated consensually? When there's no other option, 'consensual' no longer has meaning."

"Exactly," Emma said. "Fuck him or I'm going to cut his balls off right now."

She said it so matter-of-factly a chill crimped the flesh on my spine.

Emma would do exactly what she said. There was no reason to think she wouldn't.

I approached the bed.

Am I really going to do this? Am I going to fuck Colin right here in this room in front of Emma and Gabi?

It's a celebration of the matriarchy. Girl power!

I undid the top button of my jeans.

No. This was insane. Emma had gone crazy, influenced by these psychotic cult women who were hunting men and gelding them.

You mean the old pedophile who put his hands on you? Is that the poor victim you mean?

I undid the next button and the next.

Guess I'm insane now too.

Sweat beaded on Colin's chest. His hands were turning bluish gray.

I couldn't do this. I couldn't rape him.

Emma moved beside me. On the opposite side, the garden shears and the metal tray it was on gleamed.

"The sexual predators were first," Emma said. "This is the next stage. The preemptive stage. Stop them before they can traumatize a woman, or a little girl." She spit on Colin's face. He recoiled, shaking his head rapidly back and forth.

"Colin is not a molester. Not a rapist."

"Not yet. Inside every man is a toxic male."

"You're wrong."

Emma sighed and moved around me to get to the head of the bed. She yanked the sopping gag from Colin's mouth.

He took a chest-swelling breath, his Adam's apple bulging, and screamed.

"You fucking bitch! You dirty cunt! I'll kill you! I'll fucking kill you!"

Emma slapped him.

"I'll kill you, you crazy fucking slut!!!"

Emma wrangled the gag back in place, muffling his screams but they were still quite loud and you could easily make out the curses and epithets.

"See?" she said. "All you have to do is apply the right amount of pressure. All men eventually break and their true self is revealed. It takes a lot less than you think to unleash that inner toxic monster."

She patted his chest and he screamed even louder, veins zigzagging in his cheeks, whole body pulling against the restraints.

"I really need to get a ball gag. More sanitary too."

"Of course he's saying those things. Look what you did to him."

"It's in times of great distress when the true self is revealed. This is who he is. Who *every* man is."

"Emma," I said, calm as I could. "This isn't right. This has to stop."

"I'm trying to help you. But you don't even know what that means, do you? You've never cared enough to want to help me."

"What? Em—"

"I know you're not a virgin."

My mouth opened for nothing but air.

"Cocoa Beach. That night you stormed out because Colin wanted to fuck and you didn't. I saw you when you came back. You thought we were all just drunken idiots, but I saw you. And I saw the truth of it in your face."

I stared.

"When I read that story, I knew I was right. I *know* I'm right. I was raped, and I know you were too. A woman who knows, *knows.*"

How could Emma be so perceptive and I hadn't the faintest idea about what might have happened to her?

Her next words were my answer.

"You know what writers are good at? Telling lies, and the biggest ones they tell are to themselves. You fill your head with so many lies you can't even see the truth when it's right in front of you. Give us the truth, Haley. The *real* truth."

There's a form of therapy known as shock inundation treatment. It's based on the idea that the best way to make anyone confront a past trauma is to shock it to the surface, create an earthquake that frees it from the subconscious as opposed to the typically tedious slow excavation of such trauma.

For this to work, you have to create the right strenuous scenario. I'm sure no therapist ever created one quite like this.

But it worked.

This is the truth: Mr. Sams had done a lot more than just touch me. He'd made me touch him. Uncle Max hadn't only propositioned me. He'd forced me to my knees. And the teens on the beach? They weren't vampires, but they *were* monsters. It was so much worse than I've shared. So much worse. They held me down. *Ripe cunt,* the boy said, over and over as the tide rose higher and higher around me.

"Fine! Yes! You're right!"

"Say it!"

"It happened. You're right."

"Say it!"

"*I was raped!*"

Emma put her head on my back and the gesture was so gentle and sweet and surprising that tears blurred my vision.

I wept and my best friend hugged me as we stood before my naked, tied-up boyfriend.

I told you I was fucked up.

Gabi was making an almost orgasmic moan and clapping. "This is what it's all about," she cried. "Women together. *Healing!*"

"I'm proud of you," Emma said. "So, so proud. Now, it's time to take back what men have taken from you. And the only way is to take it back violently."

"I can't. Not to Colin. He's done nothing wrong."

"They're all the same," Emma said, head still on my back so her voice vibrated into my chest. "No matter what you want to think. Stripped to their core, all men are—"

"Little boys with adult desires," I said.

"Exactly. People want to think it's the penis but it's really the balls. Neuter the man and the problem is solved."

Then Emma took something off the metal tray and held it out. Three thick rubber bands.

"Wrap it tight. Easier for a clean cut."

He flinched from my touch and I flinched too, but I didn't stop. Any hesitation now and I'd never be able to do it.

His scrotum was bunched tight against his body so I had to grip it with one hand as I worked the rubber bands around it with the other and then twisted and looped the bands tighter, rolling them over his testicles into position. His engorged dick was enflamed purple-crimson.

Colin grunted and hissed and tried to throw his body free.

"The Gelder strikes again. Like he's a horse. Yeah, he wishes," Emma said as if lost in her own thoughts. Probably was. "The Gelder? Should've been The Castrator or The Neuterer or The Eunuch Maker. Or the De-Baller! Or," she propped her chin on my shoulder, "The Scrotum Snatcher!"

"Done," I said.

Emma leaned forward, our ears rubbing together.

"Very good. Grab the shears."

I did. I palmed the rubber grips, thumbed the lock, and my fingers curled into position around the pressure. Like they wanted to be there. Like this was good and right.

"Be the avenging matriarchal god."

Even with the rubber bands wound tight, Colin's balls were bunched back against his body. He must be so terrified. More terrified than he'd ever known possible. I felt bad for him. Yet, what man ever sympathized with the constant fear women endured every day that any man might be a potential rapist?

I tugged the balls down, elongating the wrinkly skin, and slid the open mouth of the shears beneath the squeezing rubber bands.

So, here I was: a young woman with her boyfriend's scrotum in one hand and a pair of red-handled garden shears in the other.

Colin screamed through the gag and shook his body so violently the bed rocked with it. Spittle dotted his cheeks and sweat pooled in his ears.

I could do whatever I wanted.

I was in complete control.

I'd never felt so powerful.

"Do it," Emma said. "And then we'll kill him together."

"What?"

"He knows it's me," she said. "I strapped him to the bed. It's easier if we kill him and dispose of the body. Cleaner that way. But first let's get those balls."

Gabi stood at the foot of the bed. She joined her hands at her chest as if this were a heartwarming scene. "Maybe we don't have to kill him," she said. "We can make him our little eunuch pet. Put a leash on him and take him for walks."

"Em, I can't."

The open blades were the spread mouth of a smiling shark. And those blades wanted to close. To prune. To snip. To cut. To sever.

"I know!" Emma said and I almost squeezed the handles in startled reflex. "If he knows *you're* involved, you'll have no choice but to help me kill him!"

She let go of me and reached over the boxspring for the sleep mask.

The rest happened very quickly.

I grabbed Emma's arm and yanked her back, the sleep mask pulling askew, one of Colin's eyes blinded in the light, and I swung the garden shears at her face. I was hoping one good slash would be enough to end this madness as quickly as possible. Didn't work. For one, the blades are not exposed like a knife would be. Two, she fell back out of the way, yanking from my grip, and crashed into the folding tray, spilling everything and her on top of it.

Gabi snagged a handful of my hair and snapped my head to the side. It would've worked perfectly, knocking me to the ground and damn near scalping me, but my arm swung directly at her and the momentum was more than enough to make her let go when the shears smashed into her face.

She didn't fall, though, but I didn't hesitate.

I stabbed the larger curved blade into her left eye.

Gabi's eye exploded in a gelatinous splash and she froze mannequin-stiff. Too shocked to react. I let go of the shears. They jutted from the eyehole a moment and fell. Clattered at my feet. She was making a low moaning, whining sound, louder and louder.

Her hands lunged for me.

A wasp stung my neck.

But it wasn't a wasp. It was a needle.

My legs turned wobbly and night fell.

"Easy, girl," Emma said. "This stuff works fast."

Blackout.

PART FIVE: UNSEX ME HERE

55

SCENE 8
An interrogation room.

HELGA sits at a long metal table. She is hand-cuffed to the table. The DETECTIVE sits across from her.

DETECTIVE: We can do this all night. You will tell me what happened.

HELGA: Look like the innocent flower, but be the serpent under it.

DETECTIVE: This isn't some stupid play. This is real life. We're talking murder.

HELGA: The raven himself is hoarse that croaks the fatal entrance of Duncan under my battlements.

The DETECTIVE is too annoyed to continue. He gets up, walks out.

HELGA addresses the audience or maybe it's the

WHAT EVER HAPPENED TO JO ROSE?

imaginary one in her mind . . .

HELGA: Oh, I'll tell you what happened. You people in the dark. You've always been there for me. You beautiful people! (Pause) You wouldn't judge me. You love me. Real, pure love. No love is more pure than that of you adoring people in the dark. (Pause) Oh, I've been bad. There were so many. But you'd never punish me. They were all bad men. You know I did it all for you. I did it for love. And I'd do it again. And again. (Pause) They had it coming. Deserved it. (Pause) And when I cried, 'Come, thick night, and pall thee in the dunnest smoke of hell, that my keen knife see not the wound it makes' heaven did not peep through the blanket of the dark to cry, 'Hold, hold.'

56

AN AIRY AND EXCITED *COOU!-COOU!* sound like something from a cartoon with adventurous mice and predatory cats brought me blinking back into the moment.

My head hangover-throbbed and my neck hurt like I'd slept on it wrong.

A white-slathered face with thick red lips and eyes peering through big, winged eyelashes beneath a black wig leaned toward me across the kitchen table. A Kabuki nightmare: Ms. Rose in fully costumed regalia, butterfly kimono, fake nails, the makeup like stucco plaster.

Behind me, the cuckoo clock ticked the seconds.

"Ms. Rose—"

"No, *dahhhling.*"

"Jo—"

"I'm Helga. Helga the Hag. Don't I look marvelous?" She was in full dramatic mode, gesticulating and emotive, her voice loud, each word played to the audience in the upper mezzanine. "It's time for my greatest performance!"

The Royal typewriter was between us, the typed pages beside it.

My mouth tasted cottony dry. I started to speak, stopped.

There were other people in the house. Lots of them. In the other rooms, they were talking and laughing and moving around.

Not that I could be sure, yet I was—it was the women from the shelter next door.

From the cult.

"I'm going to tell you a story," Ms. Rose said, "and then show you something and then we've got writing to do."

I stopped shaking my head because it felt like the room might collapse into the ground. Or my head might.

I tried standing and fell back into the chair.

"You're not going anywhere," Emma said. She stood at the door to the outside. She'd exchanged the scrubs for a sparkly flapper dress that showed off the triple moon tattoo at her collarbone. She wore matching opera gloves up to her elbows and a feathered hairband across her forehead and strap pumps on her feet.

"Costume party?" I asked.

"More like a little girl's birthday party," Emma said. "The way you dressed."

Only then did I feel the chiffon and satin folds of the pink princess gown I was wearing. They'd stripped me and put me in this hideous thing. I reached up and tugged at the plastic tiara tangled in my hair but it was stuck. They'd put makeup on me too, and I smeared my hand down my cheek. My palm glittered.

"You think this is funny?"

Before the Final Girl takes an ax to the sadist's crotch in *Cabin Girls*, she's forced to put on a little girl's pink princess outfit.

"You sure do look purdy," Emma saying the hillbilly's line.

"It's a celebration, *dahhhling*," Ms. Rose said. "A magical night."

She touched my arm and I pulled away so hard it flung behind me into the wall.

"No reason to be dramatic," Ms. Rose said. "Will you listen?"

In Emma's hands, the box containing the garden shears.

"Colin?" I asked.

Emma gave me a come-hither expression, even licking her lips for good measure. "Exactly where we left him . . . Though he's a bit more uncomfortable now."

"No . . ."

"Yes."

"You . . . ?"

"Inside every man is a toxic male, until you remove his manhood."

I was going to vomit. I felt it.

"What's a man without his balls?" Ms. Rose said. "I call it an improvement."

"You're crazy," I said. Except even as I said it, I couldn't say the rest of it—*Both of you are crazy*—because the truth was more encompassing: *Both of you are crazy and I'm crazy too*.

"Maybe, darling, maybe." She shifted in her chair, sat taller. Her face went slack and then crimped back to life. *She's becoming a character*. "You're the one stabbing people in the eye. All we're doing is cutting off some balls."

"You're lucky I'm a nurse," Emma said. "But Gabi's pissed."

"Let me go."

"Afraid not. You're with us."

Her grin was the hillbilly's.

"My real name is Didi Monroe," Ms. Rose said. "A humble girl summoned by the acting gods to grace the stage and the silver screen. I was a starlet. I played the ingenue and then the seductress and finally the hag. That's how it goes. They love you when you're young and supple and then they relegate you to the aging temptress and then they vilify you as the crone."

Jo was either playing a role within a role—Ms. Rose as Helga as performed by Didi—or she was completely insane.

Maybe all of the above.

"But Didi knew just what to do. When that awful producer took advantage of her, she schemed her revenge, and eventually she got her vengeance. Didi Monroe always knows just what to do."

I thought I understood, or at least saw how I could write her story. When Sylvan rapes Jo, her mind splits to protect her from the trauma, and from this moment of depersonalization a new identity is born. The fearless Didi Monroe. And it is Didi who gets her revenge on Sylvan years later in an L.A. motel.

"But even Didi is no match for the horrors of age!" Ms. Rose flipped her hands over her head and cocked her hips back and forth to catch the hands as they fluttered down. "Should I be reviled as a sexual creature? After what age should women be stigmatized for their sexual cravings?"

Just as Emma had done, Ms. Rose curled her tongue across her red lips. She leaned toward me again. Her face made me think of demonic clowns.

"Why is it so bad that I should want to fuck?"

Laughter scattershot from her mouth so hard and loud I was jolted.

WHAT EVER HAPPENED TO JO ROSE?

"Men get to fuck whoever they want, regardless of age," Emma said. "Why shouldn't we?"

"You're making a grand statement against the patriarchy? That it?"

"An old man can shove his dick in a teenage girl and society applauds," Emma said, "but an old woman wants some young cock and he'll run for the bathroom to puke. So, yeah, fuck the patriarchy."

"Men? Women? Doesn't matter," Ms. Rose said. "*Age*. That's what matters. Getting old is awful. It's debilitating and humiliating and disgusting. You liberal girls get in a tizzy because of problematic stereotypes, but that's because you look in the mirror and you see young flesh, perky tits, a firm ass. Just wait, honey. Just you wait. Both of you. Time is going to ravage you. Ageism? Sexism? You think it can be different? You think society can change? You want to blame men for how we look at old women? No man ever looked at an old woman with more disgust than she looked at herself. It isn't society. Not cultural norms. It's the body. It betrays you. It sabotages you. You believe an old woman can be sexy? You think you know. You don't know shit." Her smile was hideous in its madness. "Just you wait. The truth is going to kill you."

As if on cue, applause sounded like fireworks in the other room.

And behind me, the clock sprang out to sing its call. This time *coou!-coou!* sounded like *uh-oh! uh-oh!*

57

I NEEDED TO GET OUT of here. Go to the police. I'd have to confess that yes, my fingerprints were on the garden shears, that yes, my hand was on them when the blades severed Mr. Sams's manhood, that yes, I had a clear motive to do it but no, it wasn't my idea and no, I didn't *want* to do it and no, I didn't do it willingly.

Except . . .

Except, when Emma's gloved hand slipped over mine and squeezed, I hadn't resisted. Hadn't even tried to. I needed only the slightest push from her and I applied the rest of the pressure. I severed the skin and the blood vessels and the nerves, what's called the spermatic cord; it was my hand squeezing so tight the blades snipped it all as easily as scissors through paper and string.

I'm guilty. I'm a criminal. I sexually mutilated a man.

These thoughts should've left me cold but they didn't. They didn't because they felt right.

This is who I am now.

"Are you listening, darling?"

"Yes," I said. I felt suddenly calm. My breathing was steady, my head clear.

"His name was Harvey Weiner. How perfect is that?"

"Who is Harvey?"

167

"My boarder," she said as if that should be apparent.

I did have a boarder, she'd said. *Young man. Transient, I think. He kept to himself. Prurient interests, was rather distasteful, unfortunately.*

"I normally wouldn't, of course, but it was Christmas time and I was feeling rather Christian. Funny, yes? He looked like a stray dog, skinny and shivering. So haggard. My heart broke for him."

She stood quickly, taking center stage, and as she spoke she acted it out.

He knocked on my door and said, 'I hear you'd be . . . amenable,' really focusing on that word like a child sounding out as he reads aloud, 'to someone staying with you.' I looked him up and down and said, 'This is no flop house, though it may have been a den of ill repute for a short time.'"

She laughed a full belly of false-sounding jocularity. Playing it up for me, her audience.

"Well, I might have been Christian but this man was not very Christian at all. He was profane and rude and unclean. He smelled. Never trust a man who smells. I should've known. I don't mean the oniony body odor stink of a lingering sweat, either. His stink was the salty spume stench all men like he emanate. They reek of their man juice. Like it's seeping out their pores. Bad enough to make me ill. When you're an old woman like me you know how to recognize the wickedness of a man's heart by the cum-stink of his flesh."

She was playing it up even more. Every line punctuated with theatrical elan. She stared wide-eyed. Flared her nostrils. Her hands floated and sawed and swept.

"A woman warned you about me, didn't she?"

Stay away! She's bad! Bad!

"I know she did. It's okay. Her name is Victoria Weiner. His wife, that's right. I didn't know then, of course. He pretended to be a transient so he could spy on her and when he got the chance, he attacked.

"Poor girl was outside taking some sun and he assaulted her. No yelling, no argument. He hit her and hit her and hit her and fled back here just as the women were about to stop him."

"That's when I, Didi Monroe, got the most wonderful, glorious idea."

Jo hunched over, arching her shoulders and making her hands into claws, and stalked toward me very, very slowly.

"I seduced him. Yes, I did. And he was more than willing. He was full of violent lust from beating his wife. Physical violence or sex, it's all the same to men. It's all aggression.

"And when I had him with his pants around his ankles, I thwacked him with the bust of the Bard himself. Thought I'd killed him. He lay flat, blood seeping from his ear."

She stopped within a foot of me, so close her breath was on my face.

"He wasn't dead. But I bet he wishes he were."

She hugged herself so the kimono cocooned around her in layers and she bent as if bowing before me. Her laughter started as a quiet jittering hum and then a tittering chortle and it got louder and louder and she rose to full height and her whole body quivered out that mad cackle and she stepped back and spread her arms, unfurling enormous butterfly wings patterned with dazzling predatory eyes and her laughter echoed all around as if born from the very walls of this house.

"That poor woman thinks *I'm* dangerous. *Ha.* It was her husband who was the danger. I saved her from him. He's no threat to her anymore. Or to anyone. She isn't right in the head. Traumatic brain injury from the assault. Nothing we can do about that but be kind to her and understanding. As for Harvey . . . Well, there's *plenty* we can do to him."

"What did you do?"

"Oh, darling, it's glorious."

58

MS. ROSE HELD OUT HER hand as if to a lover and I got to my feet and took it.

She led me out of the kitchen and into the main area where both sitting rooms were filled with people standing around as if at a party. All the candles were lit, dozens and dozens of them, wax dripping from a ceiling chandelier, flickering shadowy light in every direction among the people. Maybe it was as few as fifteen or as many as thirty, but it felt cramped with people, considering they'd all somehow wedged themselves among the furniture and antiques.

All of them women and all in costume.

It was a madhouse of playing dress-up. Gowns and evening dresses and cocktail dresses, sparkly with sequins and rhinestones, and women in black slips and several in pinafore dresses little girls might wear and strapless dresses and sundresses with flower patterns and one woman in a ballgown of glittering gold and white fit for a queen.

Their faces were made-up, several wore wigs, and most women were in heels.

"Good evening, ladies," Ms. Rose said.

They fell silent, turned toward us from both rooms.

"I present to you, Haley Fields."

She raised my arm and led me forward a few steps and turned me. I was now before them, my back to the front door, the staircase ahead.

Emma stood directly across from me holding the box.

Something happened then I'm not sure I can explain. Call it realization or epiphany or hysteria.

What I saw in her face then was not madness or murder. It was love.

She loved me and that's why she'd done it.

She'd planned all of this. Getting me to visit Ms. Rose, me reading her my stories, and her blue-gloved hand sliding over mine to tell me it was okay, she would help me, that's what friends were for. She helped me get vengeance on Mr. Sams. Helped me be brave. She'd done it all for me because she was my friend.

I felt the tears and didn't wipe at them.

"She has given blood," Ms. Rose said. "She has purged. She has thrice testified. She is cleansed."

I thought of how her lips had been moving while I'd read to her. I'd thought she might be repeating my words, following along, but she'd really been reciting some incantation, magic words to prepare me for what was next. An initiation.

"Rejoice and welcome her in the name of the matriarchal god!"

The women replied in unison: *"Nothing is greater than woman!"*

"We honor the woman within and we praise the matriarchal god," Ms. Rose said.

"Nothing is greater than woman!"

"We welcome Haley Fields. She is woman!"

"Nothing is greater than woman!"

"Now," Ms. Rose said, "the blood offering."

The group to the left parted and there was the mural of Lady Macbeth and in the candlelight she flickered from one side of the fireplace to the other, just as she had when I thought I was seeing things.

Three women cloaked in black like the weird sisters themselves emerged as if from the wall and moved through the crowd, stopping at each woman, taking a hand, and slicing a palm with a razored fingernail.

"Now, darling," Jo said, "taste of each one and mine last."

Before I could think (or perhaps make a run for it), a hand floated up into my face and I saw the small red mouth in the palm a moment before it was pressed to my mouth.

I didn't recoil, didn't shove the hand away, didn't move my head. I licked the wound.

It tasted of salt.

That hand pulled away and another swam up in the flickering light. I licked the blood. And another hand. And another.

Some blood was salty like the first, others tasted metallic or even sweet like juice squeezing from a bite of ripe strawberry.

Some hands smelled of perfume and moisturizer, others were soft as cashmere or callused rough sandpaper.

This is a cult, I thought. *And now I'm a member.*

How many hands? How much blood?

I don't know.

What I do know is that as I licked blood from each palm, I felt a sense of belonging, of rightness, of sisterhood.

Were we vampires? Witches?

No, we were women.

They spoke as one: "Come, you spirits that tend on mortal thoughts, unsex me here, and fill me from the crown to the toe top-full of direst cruelty!"

Shakespeare. Fucking Shakespeare.

"Come to my woman's breasts, and take my milk for gall, you murdering ministers, wherever in your sightless substances you wait on nature's mischief!"

Blood wet my lips and chin.

Another palm and another.

"Make thick my blood; Stop up the access and passage to remorse, that no compunctious visitings of nature shake my fell purpose, nor keep peace between the effect and it!"

Then Emma was in front of me.

I took her hand in both of mine and brought it to my lips. Kissed it. Licked her blood.

It's what friends are for.

Ms. Rose was last and she stood before me with all that thick makeup making her into something larger than life, a creation for the stage, a creature to endure in the imagination.

I reached for her hand but she stopped me, leaned forward, and licked my chin and lips in a slow, smooth taste.

We kissed. Her lipstick was waxy slick. It was as sensual as any kiss I'd ever experienced.

I would've kept kissing her if she hadn't stopped me.

"Come, thick night, come," she said directly to me as the women all around us said it at the same time. "Come! *Come! COME!*"

Jo raised her hands and pierced her palm with one sharp forefinger nail, just as she had done to me on my first visit.

"Yet, here's a spot," she said.

"Shakespeare," I murmured and tasted her blood.

Like aged wine.

Or maybe I'd completely lost it. Seduced by and into madness. Maybe all of us are lost and looking for our tribe (or coven), and it doesn't matter what it is or who's in it so long as we belong.

Or I'm just more fucked up than I thought.

"We are one!" Ms. Rose yelled.

"*Nothing is greater than woman!*" the others shouted.

And I did too.

Ms. Rose touched my shoulders and I thought she might kiss me again. I would've welcomed it.

"Now, it's finally time for you to see what I've been keeping upstairs."

59

MS. ROSE LED THE WAY, me behind her, Emma behind me, the others following. Several women carried lit candles so shadows stretched and warped across the faded wallpaper.

Boxes and furniture lined the hallway on the second floor. We walked single file, sidling and wedging our way. The doors to all the rooms were closed.

Down the hall we went until we reached a small riser of steps and another closed door. A large "X" carved into the wood.

Jo ascended the steps and turned to face us. The flickering light deformed her face into a thing lumpy, crooked, reptilian.

"I'm no Dr. Frankenstein, but I have created quite the monster."

A few women giggled.

"Then again, it's easy to make a monster when you start with one. All men are monsters."

Some applauded.

"It's how they're made. But we can fix that, can't we?"

"Yes!" a few of them said.

"We know the source of their monstrousness. *It's in their balls!*"

The women erupted in cheers and applause and even whistles.

"I don't even know how I got the idea. It just *came* to me!"

Laughter like we were at a comedy club.

"Maybe it was momentary madness. An old hag going berserk. I thought I'd killed him. Cracked his pea-brained skull wide open. But I hadn't. He wasn't dead. But he was a monster and a monster needs to be neutered!"

More applause, cheers and someone even shouted, "Cut those balls!"

"They'd want me in a straitjacket for what I did. His were the first. I used the first thing I could find. Garden shears. The same ones we used today!"

She laughed in high-pitched cackles. But she wasn't crazy. Not simply crazy, anyway. She was playing a role. Maybe she was Helga channeling Didi or Jo Rose by way of Lady Macbeth.

All the world's a stage, after all.

"Hush, hush, sweet *dahhhling*." She dragged it out as usual, croaking hoarsely in a smoker's husky voice. I could picture her as one of Hollywood's first grand dames, delivering innuendo-loaded come-ons between puffs from a cigarette in one of those long holders. "Call me a fanatic, *puhhleezze*. But I'm really a crusader. We all are! It's time for the big reveal! Time for the climactic moment of *What Ever Happened to Helga the Hag?* She went batty, of course! Maybe we should call it, *What's the Matter with Didi? Or Josephine?* Or whoever I am!" A full-throated laugh ripped from her throat. It sounded painful. "You want to know what happened to me? I went *craaayyyzzzeee!*"

She paused, composing herself as the great actress she was, and grabbed the door handle.

"Welcome to the main stage, darling!"

She opened the door to the witch's hat and entered.

60

I TRIED TO SEE WHAT was waiting in there without moving but the candlelight couldn't penetrate the darkness.

The women behind me were whispering and giggling, little girls with a secret.

"What's in there?" I asked.

"Harvey," Emma said. "Go look."

The steps creaked beneath me and I entered the room. Ms. Rose was to my left moving something around, but I heard something else too—a soft moaning whimper.

Was that the sound I'd heard all the way downstairs?

I took another tentative step. Women were giggling.

It smelled of locker room maleness, humid sweat and wet dog.

Blinding white light exploded inside the room.

Ms. Rose stood beside a theater follow spot. It was one of those giant bulky things on a stand made for following a performer on stage.

Ready for your close-up, Mr. DeMille?

The room was small, pentagon shaped with thick curtains hanging from the opposite two walls that met in a "V" and set right in the middle was a genuine Frankenstein's monster hinged table tilted to showcase the man belted to it.

If you could even call it a man.

Harvey was completely naked with IV tubes in his bone-thin arms and a thicker tube dangling from his midsection like an extra penis. Head shaved to a bloody sheen, body emaciated to the skeleton, he was a brutal horror on which boils and bruises swelled and, beneath the straps cinching him in, his chest rose and fell in frantic, chaotic bursts. The intense light blanched him into an albino creature. His fingers were hacked to cauterized, useless nubs. They squirmed. His feet were missing entirely, the fleshy pink stumps raw and tender. His manhood was also completely removed. Between his legs an ugly, jagged scar oozed greenish-brown puss.

Yet even that wasn't the horror.

The *real* horror.

Emma stepped next to me. She nudged me with the wooden box. "You can help me add the new ones."

Ms. Rose yanked jutting nobs on the follow spot to make the light bright and concentric.

You'd be blinded if you stared into that light.

Not that Harvey could see, whether he had eyes or not.

Over each eye draped a scrotum.

Another dangled from each ear and one flopped from his chin. Two more sagged from his nipples.

They were grayish, wilty sacks. The skin stretched and withered. One shriveled and ancient, another taffy-melted and wobbly flaccid. Brown-tinted wrinkled skin on one. Fleshy pink on another. Pubic hair tufted stiff like dried straw off one and slicked wet on the next. Curlicues of red hair frilled another. The severed ends of each scrotum were curled dried scabs above the thick black "X" stitches holding them in place.

Harvey quivered, moaning, lips trembling.

The ballsacks shook. Gray, veiny sags.

The left testicle hung lower than the right on each one, and for a moment that detail pulled my focus. Was that how it was for all men?

"One should go on his throat," Emma said, like we were evaluating a decorated Christmas tree. "I'll stitch it right through his Adam's apple. Or maybe one in each palm. Men are always touching themselves. Not that he has fingers anymore."

I couldn't speak.

"Or you choose," Emma said. "They're both for you."

She opened the box.

177

You know what was inside. One was Mr. Sams' and one was Colin's. An old one and a young one. Sams's lay like a dead thing yanked desiccated from lifeless dirt while Colin's flared swollen red and seeped bloody gray fluid, a fresh kill.

Was Colin dead?

The question refused to be voiced.

"Isn't it stunning?" Ms. Rose said, standing beside me. "Meet Caliban."

"Shakespeare," I said, my voice finally working but sounding miles away. Caliban was a mutant slave in *The Tempest*, the Bard's final play. *You taught me language,* he says to his master, *and my profit on it is I know how to curse.* How apt. If ever there was a time to vomit or faint or suffer a panic attack, this was it.

"Uh-oh, you look a bit *peek-id.* If there were more room in here, I'd get a fainting couch. They really were known by that. It's the corsets. You can't breathe. It'd be lovely, though. You could lounge comfortably like a swooning Victorian. And admire my creation."

I wanted to pass out. *Hoped* I'd pass out.

But I wasn't going to.

Actually, I felt almost completely calm.

Because you're in shock, a voice argued.

No. I wasn't.

The only shock was that I felt fine.

"Men have been imprisoning us since caveman days," Emma said. "Isn't it great to get a little revenge? I call him The Emasculated. Funny, right?"

"He stays like this?" I asked.

"Don't feel bad for him. Sometimes I let him wander. He can't walk anymore. But he can crawl. Up and down the hall. All those scrotums swaying. And he can make sounds, though he can't speak. Hard to do without a tongue!" She cackled mad laughter. Her throat bulged with it. "That's what you were hearing the other night. Him crawling around making his little noises. Like a blind, injured puppy. So sad. But good to get some exercise!"

She went to him. Patted his head.

The spotlight baked her pancaked-white face like ceramic in a kiln. Her whole body glowed so she was a stained glass angel descending from Heaven.

"There's an idea," Emma said, "stitch one where his tongue used to be."

Ms. Rose caressed the ballsack wobbling from his ear. Fondled it. "This one's beginning to rot," she said. "It stinks!"

Her hand clenched the sack and squeezed the testicles. Mucusy slime dribbled.

"Men are so proud to have balls," Ms. Rose said. "They should display them all the time!"

A woman screamed in the hall.

Then they were all screaming. And I heard a familiar voice shouting through it.

A man's voice.

61

BEFORE I GOT IN THE white van with Gabi, before I blinded her in one eye, before I licked blood off dozens of women's palms, before I was shown the monstrous thing in the attic, I texted Dad. Two words, but it was all that was needed.

Save me.

Women pushed into the room. They shoved each other. Someone tripped, and another woman toppled forward into Harvey, her face squishing into his ruined groin.

"*Where's my daughter? Haley!*"

"*Dad!*"

He pushed his way into the room. In his khakis and chambray shirt, he was an everyman working stiff but in his hands he gripped his shotgun and that made him believe he was John Wayne. Minus the cowboy hat.

The other women in the room wedged themselves against the walls. With everyone in dresses and makeup and wigs, this moment was something surreal and insane.

"Ugh, Jesus Christ!" Dad said. "What the hell is that?"

Ms. Rose flapped her arms so the kimono unfurled into full butterfly-wing spread. *Cannibalistic vampire butterfly,* I thought. Then she screeched and ran at my father, her hands hooked into claws, her face unhinged in a crazed rictus, the theater spotlight burning her …

"*I AM WOMAN!!!*"

Her chest exploded.

Blood splattered all over Harvey.

She collapsed in a dead flop, just out of the spotlight.

The shotgun blast reverberated for several seconds, numbing the air, and then the women screamed and fled.

Dad stepped aside.

In a rush of howling wind, they all ran away.

Except for Emma.

She stood across the room opposite me, Dad between us.

On his Frankenstein table, Harvey moaned and struggled helplessly against the straps.

"What in the hell happened here? What is this?"

"Dad," I said stepping forward. "I know it looks really insane."

"Looks? *It is!*" He still couldn't process what he was seeing. Had he even realized he'd murdered someone? He looked pale, sweaty. His hands readjusted on the shotgun.

"Mr. Fields," Emma said.

Dad turned, surprised, and Emma dropped the wooden box. Its contents tumbled out.

"What have you done?" He turned to me. "*What did you do?*"

"Dad, it's okay."

"*Okay?!?*"

"Some things are not black and white. It's not that simple."

"Why the hell not?"

"Sorry, Mr. Fields, but you shouldn't have come here."

From a pocket in her flapper dress she removed the garden shears.

"Emma, don't," I said.

"He's a man, Haley. Like all the rest of them." The blades opened. "What father wouldn't sacrifice his balls for his little girl?"

"Emma, please—"

She attacked.

The shotgun blast stole the scream from my throat and my best friend from my life.

Instead of cratering her chest as the first shot had to Ms. Rose, this one obliterated Emma's right arm. White bone jutted from straggles of bleeding flesh.

Dad dropped the shotgun. His faced was dead white. His mouth opened but no sound came out.

I ran to Emma and dropped beside her.

"I was trying to help you," Emma said. Part of her ear was torn off and her neck skinned to the artery. "You needed to face the truth and take back your life."

"I know."

"It's what friends are for."

"It's okay. It's going to be okay."

"It's all book material, right?" Blood wet her lips, trickled onto her chin.

I didn't know where or if I should touch her. I fumbled for my phone but it was gone.

Emma was shaking her head. "I saw your text. I knew he would come here. To save you."

She coughed a glob of blood. It covered her tattoo. A spasm seized her against the wall.

"I'm going to save you."

Her eyes found me and she smiled.

"Dad, call 9-1-1! *Dad!*"

He didn't respond.

"Hey," Emma said. "How's the box?"

"Don't," I said. "Please."

She waved a finger at me. "You're supposed to say, 'Tight.'"

"Help! *Dad! Help!*"

But he was standing stunned, face blank, hands empty.

After we watched *Cabin Girls*, we fell asleep cocooned in that comforter. I woke sometime later to Emma's quiet crying. I hugged her close. A scary movie, that's all. But we know better, don't we? I quoted a line from the movie. It's when one of the girls has completely given up and begs to die next.

"Hey," I said to Emma, repeating the line from the movie that I'd whispered to her a decade ago in the night, "We're Cabin Girls forever. Right?"

Emma closed her eyes, slouched farther.

"No, no, no. *Emma, no!*"

Her lips were moving. I leaned close.

"I like 'em tight," she said.

PART SIX:
THE FINAL GIRL

62

HERE'S THE THING—I WAS a timid girl who'd been abused, but I'm not that girl anymore.

She'll always be with me. That scared little girl is stuck forever on the gym mat with Mr. Sams breathing down on her, but maybe that girl finally has some hope. Maybe if she looks past him she'll see me standing tall, unafraid, and in my hands a pair of red-handled garden shears.

Every little girl should have a protector.

~

I finally watched *What Ever Happened to Baby Jane?* It's melodramatic, over-the-top, and damn good. Bette Davis and Joan Crawford are mesmerizing. It's considered the best of what's known as the hag-sploitation genre, or psycho-biddy if you want to be crass.

I've been thinking about *Helga the Hag*. I'm thinking it deserves an ending. I think I'm ready to write it.

No lies necessary.

Only truth.

~

You should be afraid of old women, Ms. Rose said.

Maybe you should be afraid of all women.

~

WHAT EVER HAPPENED TO JO ROSE?

Colin's balls were reattached.

It was too late for Mr. Sams.

~

Colin won't talk to me.

I don't blame him. He must be so embarrassed.

But sometimes I wonder . . .

I think of how the sleep mask was yanked askew on his face. How he might have glimpsed something.

How he might have seen things he shouldn't have.

~

Gabi won't talk to me, either.

But she still comes to the library. Trying to finish her thesis.

Sometimes I catch her peering over a stack of books at me.

One-eyed.

~

The women's shelter must've shut down, condemned as a hotbed of cultish madness.

It wasn't.

The women at Ms. Rose's, all those bleeding palms, were not all the women from the shelter. And this matters too: Neither were those women *only* from the shelter.

Those women might've come from anywhere.

~

It was a beautiful warm day when I parked at the curb and knocked on the door of that candy-colored Victorian.

A sign on the door declared, WOMEN ONLY. And beneath that: *In a woman's heart is God's love.*

Maybe it is a cult, I thought. *Witches or not.*

The door unlocked and opened only far enough for one person to peer out. It was the stocky woman in the same jeans and blouse she'd been wearing when I first saw her.

"Yes?" she said.

"I'm Haley Fields, and I—"

She STOP-signed with her hand. "You were involved in that mess next door."

"Yes."

"I don't know anything about it," she said.

She started to go back inside.

"Did you ever talk to Ms. Rose?" I asked.

She hesitated. "No."

"Did you ever suspect anything was going on? I saw women dancing behind this shelter."

"I'm very busy. I have women who need real help."

"Victoria Weiner? Gabi Esposito?"

"Don't come here again."

If I persisted, would those two basketball player-sized women come out to remove me?

"I'm not upset," I said.

"Go!"

"Nothing is greater than woman," I blurted.

She considered, and her expression softened.

"I never spoke to Ms. Rose," she said. "But I did speak to Didi Monroe."

Then she closed the door, and I heard it lock.

~

I got a tattoo. A triple moon. Right below my collarbone.

Exactly where Emma had hers.

~

Shakespeare was right about each of us playing many parts.

Am I a character in a horror story? And if so, am I the hero or the monster?

~

This morning on the counter I found a news article Dad printed out. He doesn't talk about what happened or how for a short while afterword he was a local hero, the man who saved his daughter from psychos in a women's cult.

He doesn't watch John Wayne movies anymore, either.

When I asked about that, he looked at me with eyes that seemed very old and said, "The world has different heroes now."

The article headline made me chuckle.

GELDER STRIKES AGAIN.

Isn't that funny?

You know what's even funnier? The victim was Uncle Max.

Some guys have to learn the hard way.

~

Am I The Gelder?

It's not one person, never was. It's an idea. A legend. A vengeful matriarch.

Emma said The Gelder was a myth conjured into reality. An avenging spirit summoned from the very soul of woman. I like that.

WHAT EVER HAPPENED TO JO ROSE?

Sometimes I sit in my car and scream, "I am woman!" It feels good.

Sometimes I'm in empty parking lots when I do it.

I want to live in a world where an avenging matriarchal myth castrates sexual predators.

It's the only sensible response to male behavior.

~

Just yesterday, a Florida paper headline read: WOMAN ATTACKED ON BEACH.

A woman walking alone at night was assaulted and raped by a group of teens.

One of the assailants was wearing an I 🖤 Cocoa Beach shirt.

Some coincidences aren't coincidences at all.

They're destiny.

~

To get what you want in a man's world, you must think like a man.

Or to put it another way . . .

You got to grab the world by the balls.

AUTHOR'S NOTE AND ACKNOWLEDGEMENTS

1

My father loved horror. He collected horror novels and issues of *Fangoria* (they arrived sheathed in black plastic like small, flat corpses) and lots and lots of horror VHS tapes. He died when I was eleven, and I started reading those novels (which he kept organized in a coffin-shaped bookcase), ogling the gruesome pages of *Fangoria*, and watching those movies.

Oh, such an education! Such a school!

In the imaginary halls of my personal Horror High, I encountered possessed Regan (*The Exorcist*), and sleep-killer Freddy (*Nightmare on Elm Street*), and a homicidal ventriloquist (*Magic*), and a murderous monkey (*Monkey Shines*), and dozens of others that burrowed deep into my mind and gave me many sleepless nights (exploding heads in *Scanners*, creepy mind-reading kids in *Village of the Damned*, shower-slaughter in *Psycho*, the rotting tub woman in *The Shining*).

I seemingly chose these films at random.

One day it was *What Ever Happened to Baby Jane?*

I loved it immediately, this take on psychological madness, featuring two famous former Hollywood starlets I'd never encountered, tangled in a sick game of envy and torture.

It's funny, of course, me at 15 or 16 watching this movie with no preconceived notion about it or its stars, Crawford and Davis. Nor did I bring to my viewing any genre bias. I watched and relished.

I might as well self-analyze a little here.

My mother had me when she was 42. By the time I graduated high school in 1999, my mother was closer in age to that of my friends' grandparents than their parents.

Born in 1938, my mother was very much the product of an older generation, her own mother born in 1911, and I was raised to always defer to my elders, to save more money than I spent, to not publicly share what happens in the family, and to always keep my emotions in check. My mother was stoic, tough, resilient. I learned that from her, but I did witness her "snap" a few times.

She once had an all-out screaming fit in a checkout line at Kmart, shouting what sounded like garbled nonsense as she hurled dozens of plastic cups onto the floor. And I recall with perfect clarity the moment she saw her husband, my father, in his open casket at the funeral home.

My aunt helped her stagger toward the coffin and then my mother released a howling scream worthy of a Greek tragedy and was pawing at my father, crying out his name, weeping. My brother, 21 at the time, turned and fled. I was left standing alone in the doorway as my aunt tried to calm my mother who was hoisting my father from the coffin in an embrace.

It disturbs me to this day, and I can't help but wonder if that traumatic moment was what drew me in to the histrionics on display in *Baby Jane*.

If my mother could snap, well, anyone might. Even an old lady.

2

I never considered writing a hagsploitation book until just these past couple years.

I'm a high school English teacher, and I have the great joy (and burden) of trying to inspire my students through literature. Sometimes it actually works. One story that never fails is Joyce Carol Oates's "Where Are You Going, Where Have You Been?"

It's a work of terrifying magnitude with an ending that burrows deeper and deeper into the subconscious upon further reads. Reading it is a thrilling, unsettling, glorious experience, but reading it aloud to my students and actually teaching it has become equally unsettling and profoundly meaningful.

My female students, in particular, connect with teenager Connie's plight. Connie is a pretty girl and a pretty girl will sooner or later catch the attention of an unwanted male eye. That eye belongs to Arnold Friend. He is perhaps a sociopath, a rapist, a serial killer, even a demon, or merely a hallucination, but from the moment he says, "Gonna get you, baby," to the final paragraph where Connie opens the screen door of her house and steps out into all that vast land, the story is a white-knuckled read that keeps my students enraptured, making them both terrified for and infuriated by Connie.

Afterward when we discuss the story, my female students always share personal experiences that are so common and pervasive the class sometimes turns into something resembling a support group.

I'm glad. The girls need to share, and the boys need to hear it.

Consider: These are 17-year-olds who have for years already endured leering, sexual jokes, catcalling, taunts, come-ons, propositions, stalking, unwelcome touching, sexual abuse, and even assault. In most cases, they have suffered this behavior since puberty.

Occasionally a boy will defend the behavior with the old go-to: *We're just complimenting them* or the accusatory, *If they didn't want the attention they shouldn't dress like that.*

That often gets us into a discussion about school dress code, which is distinctly biased against the female body. No shoulders, no midriffs, no backs, no thighs. The most popular rationales for such keep-your-body-covered codes are exactly what you'd expect: We need to teach girls self-respect, and it's not fair to boys who just can't control themselves. Ah, boys will be boys. How nice for them to get an excuse while girls get the shame.

It's just skin, a female student once said. She argued she should be able to show her skin and boys should be able to control themselves. If that's too liberal-minded for you, maybe there's a Puritan village somewhere in the New England woods where you can live.

All of that isn't beside the point, or even secondary, because as Ms. Rose says, "We make excuses for men so they don't even have to."

Some stories I'll never forget: the student who said a 60-year-old man approached her at a gas station to ask if she was married and when she said no, I'm 17, he replied, "If you were my wife, I'd keep you locked in the basement." Then there's the students (yes, *students*, plural) who were followed by men through department or grocery stores or who worked in retail and had to endure the unwanted comments about their beauty and the even more unwanted casual touch when handing over a receipt or coffee.

And then there's the student who was propositioned by a family friend. This person offered to pay for the student's college, so long as she didn't tell her parents. The unsaid yet implied repayment was disguised as a comment about her goddess-like beauty. This situation inspired Haley Fields's "Graduation Party." I only wish my student had been able to smash a bottle over the head of that family friend as the character in Haley's story does.

Are all men monsters? No. Is there a toxic male inside every man? Well, that's like the proverb about the two wolves that live inside every person—the evil one and the good one. Which one wins? The one you feed, of course.

Connie's story confirms for many of my students that they are seen, that their experiences are validated. This is good, except the downside is so obvious it's almost too depressing: Oates's story is from 1966, almost sixty years ago; this problem with men is nothing new.

3

When I wrote *What Ever Happened to Jo Rose?* I wanted to give voice to those stories my students had shared and I wanted to give my fictional characters an opportunity at vengeance in the bloody spirit of Grand Guignol horror.

Certain motifs were unplanned. I'm thinking here of Lady Macbeth and the popularized depiction of witches, or little girl princesses, of the self-help book *Slaying the Masculine*, and Helga the Hag (an alternate title for this book, and a reference to the hagsploitation genre itself), and the victimized and tortured characters in *Cabin Girls* (which I made up but seems to me like it must exist). There's certainly a comment to be made about women in popular culture and the subsequent myths those works perpetuate, but I leave you to make your own conclusions.

I do wonder, though: Is what I've written exploitative? What right do I have to tell this story? Am I hijacking someone else's story just so I can make a few bucks?

I don't want to get on the proverbial soapbox here to preemptively defend myself, but I do want to share a basic truth I believe about writing.

It is an act of empathy.

Stephen King has said that "writing is an act of willed understanding," and I have found that to be true.

He has also said that "fiction is the truth within the lie," and that is very much true, assuming the writer is honest and fair and empathetic.

This is the first work I've ever written told first-person from a woman's perspective. I debated about that. Certainly, it was risky, and part of me feared I'd be seen as coopting something that wasn't mine, and another part of me feared I'd simply be mocked for daring to think I could do such a thing, and yet Haley wanted to tell this story in her own words. I was her conduit.

Writing is an act of empathy. It teaches you to care about other people. I cared very deeply about the characters in this story, and I hope that comes through.

I hope also I was fair to all my characters. Consider Ms. Rose. It would be easy for her to be an over-the-top stereotype, a clear homage to Bette Davis in *Baby Jane*, but I didn't want her so easily dismissed. She became a wonderfully layered character, revealing to me her many sides, be that Helga or Didi or perhaps even a few others she left unshared.

Writers have a responsibility to the truth. Have I been truthful? Have I depicted women fairly? Should any one character, female or male, in this story (or any story) be a stand-in for all such people?

Or am I trying to shield myself from any blowback?

As ever, you the reader can make your own conclusions.

4

Immense thanks and gratitude to Carrie Nicely and everyone at Grindhouse Press for believing in this story. This is the second work of mine they've published (the first, *The Hands of Onan*, is about an all-male masturbation cult and of which Ms. Rose remarks, "Men are disgusting."), and I'm honored to be in the Grindhouse stable of authors. This book is dedicated to Carrie and to my friend and colleague, Marissa Rantinella, one of the few people who has read *all* of my published works and whose encouragement and enthusiasm is greatly appreciated.

Additional shoutouts to former student and phenomenal writer

Gabriella Esposito (after whom I named a character in this tale), and to all my students who have felt comfortable enough in my class to share their experiences—know that you are seen, you are heard.

And thanks of course to Jennifer, my wife, who is unflagging in her support of this crazy writing habit that gets me up at 4 every morning.

5

Originally, this story was going to be about Emma forcing Haley to torture Colin in order to prove there's a toxic male inside every man. That moment exists in these pages, but from the beginning there was so much more to explore in this tale. These characters had more to share and I did what any responsible author should do, I let them.

I don't have any children, but if I did I'd want a daughter because I'd want to raise her to be strong and confident and unafraid. I'd tell her what I tell my female students, *Be brave.*

Of course it isn't that simple. Girls are taught early to be reserved, polite, and to always smile. Boys are permitted to be loud, to rough-house, and to take what they want. I want my female students to be brave, to believe in themselves, to speak up, but when men see themselves as wolves and women as sheep for the taking, the line between bravery and brazenness can be quite dangerous.

Is there a toxic male inside every man?

The answer is too troubling to consider.

So I think of how this story ends, and it makes me grin. Somewhere out in these dark streets riding around in a nondescript van (with a pair of neon pink truck nuts dangling beneath the license plate) is The Gelder.

Or maybe it's only a myth. Tell yourself what you want.

You may think differently when you feel the steel blades of those garden shears slide into position.

Be well, be happy, be kind.

Chris DiLeo
November 2023

Chris DiLeo is the author of twelve books, including *The Hands of Onan* from Grindhouse Press. He is also the Gross-Out Champion from AuthorCon 2 in April 2023 for his story, "Lick Your Fingers." He is a high school English teacher in New York. Connect with him @authordileo.

Other Grindhouse Press Titles

#666__*Satanic Summer* by Andersen Prunty

#102__*I Think I'm Alone Now* by Ali Seay

#101__*Cute Aggression* by Emily Lynn

#100__*Headless* by Scott Cole

#099__*The Killing Kind* by Bryan Smith

#098__*An Affinity for Formaldehyde* by Chloe Spencer

#097__*Kill the Hunter* by Bryan Smith

#096__*The Gauntlet* by Bryan Smith

#095__*Bad Movie Night* by Patrick Lacey

#094__*Hysteria: Lolly & Lady Vanity* by Ali Seay

#093__*The Prettiest Girl in the Grave* by Kristopher Triana

#092__*Dead End House* by Bryan Smith

#091__*Graffiti Tombs* by Matt Serafini

#090__*The Hands of Onan* by Chris DiLeo

#089__*Burning Down the Night* by Bryan Smith

#088__*Kill Hill Carnage* by Tim Meyer

#087__*Meat Photo* by Andersen Prunty and C.V. Hunt

#086__*Dreaditation* by Andersen Prunty

#085__*The Unseen II* by Bryan Smith

#084__*Waif* by Samantha Kolesnik

#083__*Racing with the Devil* by Bryan Smith

#082__*Bodies Wrapped in Plastic and Other Items of Interest* by Andersen Prunty

#081__*The Next Time You See Me I'll Probably Be Dead* by C.V. Hunt

#080__*The Unseen* by Bryan Smith

#079__*The Late Night Horror Show* by Bryan Smith

#078__*Birth of a Monster* by A.S. Coomer

#077__*Invitation to Death* by Bryan Smith

#076__*Paradise Club* by Tim Meyer

#075__*Mage of the Hellmouth* by John Wayne Comunale

#074__*The Rotting Within* by Matt Kurtz

#073__*Go Down Hard* by Ali Seay

#072__*Girl of Prey* by Pete Risley

#071__*Gone to See the River Man* by Kristopher Triana

#070__*Horrorama* edited by C.V. Hunt

#069__*Depraved 4* by Bryan Smith

#068__*Worst Laid Plans: An Anthology of Vacation Horror* edited by Samantha Kolesnik

#067__*Deathtripping: Collected Horror Stories* by Andersen Prunty

#066__*Depraved* by Bryan Smith

#065__*Crazytimes* by Scott Cole

#064__*Blood Relations* by Kristopher Triana

#063__*The Perfectly Fine House* by Stephen Kozeniewski and
Wile E. Young

#062__*Savage Mountain* by John Quick

#061__*Cocksucker* by Lucas Milliron

#060__*Luciferin* by J. Peter W.

#059__*The Fucking Zombie Apocalypse* by Bryan Smith

#058__*True Crime* by Samantha Kolesnik

#057__*The Cycle* by John Wayne Comunale

#056__*A Voice So Soft* by Patrick Lacey

#055__*Merciless* by Bryan Smith

#054__*The Long Shadows of October* by Kristopher Triana

#053__*House of Blood* by Bryan Smith

#052__*The Freakshow* by Bryan Smith

#051__*Dirty Rotten Hippies and Other Stories* by Bryan Smith

#050__*Rites of Extinction* by Matt Serafini

#049__*Saint Sadist* by Lucas Mangum

#048__*Neon Dies at Dawn* by Andersen Prunty

#047__*Halloween Fiend* by C.V. Hunt

#046__*Limbs: A Love Story* by Tim Meyer

#045__*As Seen On T.V.* by John Wayne Comunale

#044__*Where Stars Won't Shine* by Patrick Lacey

#043__*Kinfolk* by Matt Kurtz

#042__*Kill For Satan!* by Bryan Smith

#041__*Dead Stripper Storage* by Bryan Smith

#040__*Triple Axe* by Scott Cole

#039__*Scummer* by John Wayne Comunale

#038__*Cockblock* by C.V. Hunt

#037__*Irrationalia* by Andersen Prunty

#036__*Full Brutal* by Kristopher Triana

#035__*Office Mutant* by Pete Risley

#034__*Death Pacts and Left-Hand Paths* by John Wayne
Comunale

#033__*Home Is Where the Horror Is* by C.V. Hunt

#032__*This Town Needs A Monster* by Andersen Prunty

#031__*The Fetishists* by A.S. Coomer

#030__*Ritualistic Human Sacrifice* by C.V. Hunt

#029__*The Atrocity Vendor* by Nick Cato

#028__*Burn Down the House and Everyone In It* by Zachary T. Owen

#027__*Misery and Death and Everything Depressing* by C.V. Hunt

#026__*Naked Friends* by Justin Grimbol

#025__*Ghost Chant* by Gina Ranalli

#024__*Hearers of the Constant Hum* by William Pauley III

#023__*Hell's Waiting Room* by C.V. Hunt

#022__*Creep House: Horror Stories* by Andersen Prunty

#021__*Other People's Shit* by C.V. Hunt

#020__*The Party Lords* by Justin Grimbol

#019__*Sociopaths In Love* by Andersen Prunty

#018__*The Last Porno Theater* by Nick Cato

#017__*Zombieville* by C.V. Hunt

#016__*Samurai Vs. Robo-Dick* by Steve Lowe

#015__*The Warm Glow of Happy Homes* by Andersen Prunty

#014__*How To Kill Yourself* by C.V. Hunt

#013__*Bury the Children in the Yard: Horror Stories* by Andersen Prunty

#012__*Return to Devil Town (Vampires in Devil Town Book Three)* by Wayne Hixon

#011__*Pray You Die Alone: Horror Stories* by Andersen Prunty

#010__*King of the Perverts* by Steve Lowe

#009__*Sunruined: Horror Stories* by Andersen Prunty

#008__*Bright Black Moon (Vampires in Devil Town Book Two)* by Wayne Hixon

#007__*Hi I'm a Social Disease: Horror Stories* by Andersen Prunty

#006__*A Life On Fire* by Chris Bowsman

#005__*The Sorrow King* by Andersen Prunty

#004__*The Brothers Crunk* by William Pauley III

#003__*The Horribles* by Nathaniel Lambert

#002__*Vampires in Devil Town* by Wayne Hixon

#001__*House of Fallen Trees* by Gina Ranalli

#000__*Morning is Dead* by Andersen Prunty